LETHAL EQUITY

By VINCE AIELLO

Published by SarEth Publishing House
SarEth Publishing House
Carlsbad, California

"Joe the Lawyer" Copyright © 2015 Vincent F. Aiello. Used with permission.
Lyrics by Vince Aiello
Music by Steve Morris
Produced & Performed by Steve Morris – ToneDef Audio
http://tonedefaudio.com

Cover Art Copyright © 2015 Sarah Rose Aiello
Armorer Advisor: Ethan P. Aiello

First Edition: November 2015

Printed in the United States of America

ISBN 978-0-9883413-7-1

SPHN 15-05011505

SarEth Publishing House

Also by Vince Aiello

LEGAL DETRIMENT
THE LITIGATION GUY
LEGION'S LAWYERS
FAITH FULL

For **Glenn Edgarian**, **Paul Clifford**, & **Jim Ledakis**
– My friends, my brothers, my family.

To be feared is a powerful weapon. I realized that a law firm is like a principality. And I'm the guy who leads the army. I have to be cruel, because that's the only way I can command my lawyers' absolute respect.

-Roger Legion

Legion's Lawyers

PROLOGUE

WOODED BRUSH OFF HIGHWAY 95
ATHOL, IDAHO
THE FRIDAY BEFORE LABOR DAY

The bucolic beauty of the Coeur D'Alene National Forest, located in the Idaho panhandle, is breathtaking. It is 1,135 square miles of lush green serenity nestled around various lakes and hills that created spectacular views. The forest was filled with remnants of unused roadways that were once used to transport lumber, gold and silver out of it. Now, those roads are used for occasional recreation by people who come to fish, hunt and hike.

Even though Idaho has a reputation for producing potatoes, its nickname is the "Gem State," based on the fact that nearly every known type of gemstone has been found there. It was the pursuit of precious stones that brought many settlers to the state. They trekked upon the roads of the forest in pursuit of their fortunes.

Athol, Idaho is located approximately twenty-six miles south of Sandpoint, Idaho down US Highway 95 just outside of the Coeur D'Alene National Forest. On this day, beyond the southern city limits, white and black smoke could be seen billowing up through the trees, but from the street level, no cause or place of origin could be observed.

FBI Special Agents Brenda Tomaras and Sam Mezner were heading north in a late model Ford Explorer SUV on Highway 95, closing in on Athol, in search of a crime scene. Agent Tomaras was a sixteen-year veteran of the FBI, with four commendations for valor during her tenure. Brenda was forty-one years old, five feet one inch tall, weighing 105 pounds with crystal blue eyes. Her copper, gold-red hair gave her the nickname of 'Sparkplug' in the office. Her dogged pursuit of every perpetrator that she sought made her a one-woman wrecking machine.

Officer Mezner was twenty-eight years old, five feet eleven inches tall, and 185 pounds. He had a baby face and would not be looked to as the authority figure in a group. He had only been a field agent for the past four months and was still trying to ease into this line of work. He was often pensive and looked reverent, as if he would be offended if you even said a harsh word in his presence.

These agents were based out of the FBI Coeur d'Alene satellite office, which was under the jurisdiction of the FBI Salt Lake City Field Office. Coeur d'Alene was located approximately twenty-one miles south of Athol. The weather this day was overcast with a mild temperature of sixty-four degrees.

Both Special Agents wore blue windbreakers with large, yellow letters sewn on the back that simply stated 'FBI.'

As the city limits of Athol drew closer, they found their crime scene. Located on the eastern side of the highway were two large fire trucks: a 2012 Rosenbauer International Rescue Pumper and a 1994 E-One Custom Chassis Pumper. Both of these trucks carried one thousand gallons of water and were from the Timberlake Fire Protection District, which provided fire protection to this geographic area. Also on site were two ambulances from the Fire

Protection District, who were waiting for the firemen to conclude their work.

The scene included several state police officers directing traffic and placing bright, yellow plastic tape with the words, 'POLICE LINE – DO NOT CROSS,' printed on it and spread over a wide area.

FBI Special Agent Brenda Tomaras pulled up behind one of the pumper trucks and parked the Ford Explorer. Before they exited the vehicle, Brenda shared an admonition for her junior partner.

"Be sure you remind them that this is a federal crime scene."

"I will," Agent Mezner responded as he pulled a lanyard out of his coat that was around his neck to display his identification.

The agents got out of the vehicle and walked over to the closest Idaho State Trooper. They flashed their badges and were allowed access to the area inside the yellow tape line. They walked down a roadway that consisted of two tire lanes with lush grass between them and a fully expanded firehose through which water pumped. After several winding turns, they saw what the firemen were focusing their energy on.

There, burning, was a 2004 GMC C6500 Griffin Armored Truck. The gross weight of the vehicle was 25,500 pounds. It was operated by a company called Parapet Logistics out of Coeur d'Alene. The truck had completed a route through Sandpoint, Idaho earlier that day and was on its way back to their headquarters.

The fire coming from the truck was creating black smoke, while adjacent trees that caught fire were creating white smoke. As the two FBI agents drew closer, the fire was totally arrested. One of the firemen turned and saw the agents. He wanted to share a comment. The fireman removed his breathing apparatus to speak with them.

"Metal's not supposed to burn. It had to be doused with an accelerant."

Agent Tomaras acknowledged his comment and she looked around the truck. On the passenger side of the truck, the bullet-proof glass of the passenger window appeared pulverized and a small hole, approximately the size of a golf ball was broken through it. The hood of the truck was smashed down into the engine compartment and bent in the center, perpendicular to the windshield.

"You guys gonna move it soon?" the same fireman asked.

"We're going to have some crime lab technicians go over it first," Brenda advised.

Then a voice rang out from behind them.

"Excuse me," a state trooper called out, accompanied by a man wearing a Parapet Logistics uniform. "This gentleman is from the armored car company."

"I brought the key, if you want to get in," the uniformed man replied. He handed the key to Special Agent Mezner.

"Sam, you got gloves?" Agent Tomaras asked.

"Yeah," Agent Mezner replied.

Both FBI agents donned a pair of green, latex gloves. As Brenda was adjusting her gloves, she noticed something on the ground near the back of the armored truck. She took a pen out of her pocket and squatted down next to it. It was a red, circular reflective lens with a three-inch diameter that was cracked in the areas where it would have been screwed into a vehicle. Brenda took the pen and lifted one side of it. Agent Mezner squatted down next to her.

"We need to find the vehicle that lost this reflector," Agent Tomaras stated with certainty.

Mezner handed the key to Brenda who inserted it into the lock mechanism for the rear doors of the truck. She manipulated the key into the blackened keyhole and the clicking sound of the door could be heard.

Agent Tomaras pulled one door open and undid an internal latch to unsecure the other door. She pulled them both wide open.

The firemen, trooper, Parapet Logistics employee, and the two FBI special agents simply stared at the contents of the armored truck with various looks of amazement, shock, and disgust. It was obviously much more than just a robbery.

Part 1

CHAPTER 1

AMERICA'S FINEST CITY BUILDING, 24TH FLOOR
SAN DIEGO, CALIFORNIA
2 WEEKS EARLIER

Roger Legion's concentration on a pleading that he was perusing was suddenly interrupted by a memory from the past. The fact pattern from the case he was reading was eerily similar to one that was in his office years before. His memory was not so much about the details of the case, but of the lawyer in his office who handled it. A lawyer who was bound for greatness, but had his whole career derail in search of easy money.

Roger peered out the window of his corner office and wondered what his firm would be like if all of his fifteen lawyers had the gravitas, talent, and steel nerve of that attorney. Then, the insurance defense law firm of Legion & Associates would be a power to be reckoned with. Roger always acted as if his law firm was the best in the County of San Diego, but there were days when he had his doubts.

He pushed back from his desk and rose, still focused on the ocean in the distance outside his window. Roger Legion was in his mid-60s, six feet tall, 195 pounds, and looked twenty years younger than his actual age. He had a full head of black hair, accented with gray throughout. He wore a dark, blue custom-made suit of fine Italian fabric, with an executive, white shirt, also custom-made, and a silk, blue and black striped tie.

As he stood, like a king from his throne, he gave each of his sleeves a slight tug, and it was just enough for someone to spot his gold cuff links. The ones he wore today were engraved with the letter 'L' and contained a small diamond.

He did not want to break his gaze on the ocean, but it was time for the weekly attorney meeting. He proceeded down the western hallway of the twenty-fourth floor of the America's Finest City Building. As he reached the large conference room at the end of the hallway, adjacent to the reception area, he could hear the confluence of voices become louder.

The conference room consisted of a wall of frosted glass that separated it from the reception area. The exterior wall of the room was top-to-bottom glass that allowed for a panoramic view of the Pacific Ocean. The centerpiece of the room was the table. It was twenty-four feet long and five feet wide. It had an inlaid granite top and mahogany finish. Eighteen people could sit at the table comfortably, which allowed the entire law firm to be seated for an event.

When Roger entered the room, most of the voices lowered, but their conversations did not stop. Roger did a visual roll call of the attorneys in the room. He counted twelve attorneys, all wearing bright, white shirts and only one wearing a suitcoat. Roger Legion never removed his suit coat. He considered it to be part of a warrior's uniform that was incomplete without it. Outside the office, his attorneys would not be seen without their coats. It would be like a knight without his armor.

The voices continued to elevate as Roger concluded his attorney accounting.

"Where's Luke Cordel?" Roger made a general inquiry to the crowd, without asking anyone in particular. Most voices were still conversing when he asked this question.

Luke Cordel was an attorney who had been at the firm for the past three and one-half years. He was with Roger Legion on a day when Roger found himself in the middle of a terrorist attack on the Coronado Bay Bridge. Luke was involved in a firefight with the terrorists, while trying to save Roger, another lawyer from the firm and a paralegal, which ended when Luke was struck in the head by a bullet and lost one of his eyes.

Dennis Richards, a lawyer who had been with the firm for six years and considered himself to be somewhat of a joker, decided to chirp in to Legion's question.

"Yeah, where is Dead-eye Dick?" He asked his question to the crowd, hoping to get a roaring response.

Roger found no humor in it.

"What did you say?" Legion asked while the voices in the room elevated over his. He did catch Richards' attention.

"Nothing. Let it go," Dennis said dismissively.

"SHUT UP!" Legion blared and his voice reverberated within the room. Now, a pall of silence enveloped it.

"What did you say?" Legion again asked. His voice was meted and his ice-blue eyes locked on to Dennis Richards with laser-guided precision.

Dennis knew he could not blow him off, so he surrendered to the inquiry.

"I asked where Dead-eye Dick was." The way he uttered the words seemed to underlie that he was asking for forgiveness. Everyone in the room knew what was about to happen.

"Do you know how he lost that eye?" Roger asked Dennis rhetorically, not waiting for an answer. "He lost it saving me and two other people from this law firm that day on the bridge. Luke ran to the danger. What were you doing that day?"

Dennis stared at him like an errant schoolchild awaiting punishment.

"I was at a depo," he responded.

"So, you were pretending to be a lawyer? Right?"

Dennis did not say a word.

"You know what a deposition is if you don't go to trial?" Legion asked. "Useless. A waste of time. It's nothing more than a billing event. That's why you can send the dumbest asshole in the world to cover it and you don't miss out on anything if he screws it up."

Legion then turned his gaze to the rest of the men in the room.

"I don't ever want to hear another comment about Luke's eye. If I do, heads are going to go bouncing right out the door."

He then returned his focus to Dennis.

"Do you understand?"

"Yes," he replied timidly.

Roger then backed away from the table and walked over to the alabaster glass door through which he entered and pulled it open.

"Nina," he said capturing her attention. "We are going to start." Nina, the firm's receptionist, was the only non-lawyer on the twenty-fourth floor. Legion's voice was her cue that they were not to be disturbed. Roger Legion had set the tone for the attorney meeting.

CHAPTER 2

Roy Sims had been in charge of information technology at Legion & Associates for the past four years. He was the person you called if you had a problem with the law firm issued cell phone, your work computer, or anything else technology-related.

Roger Legion was somewhat 'old school' and did not really have an admiration nor proficiency for modern technology, but he begrudgingly forced himself to learn it and use it with the assistance of Roy.

Roy was thirty-one years old, five feet seven inches tall, and weighed 265 pounds. He was bald, with the exception of a band of hair around his skull and he wore glasses with thick, black frames. He had a cubicle on the twenty-third floor of the building, along with law clerks, paralegals, secretaries, and the accounting department of the law firm. They also had runners, who would bring anything requested by an attorney to the twenty-fourth floor. No person from the twenty-third floor was allowed on the twenty-fourth floor without a business-related reason.

Roy was the only male at Legion & Associates that was not required to wear a tie. Roger viewed his work as technical in nature and had nothing to do with the practice of law. In addition, there would never be a need for Roy to leave the office.

On this day, Roy wore blue Haggar slacks with a black belt and a periwinkle, long-sleeve button shirt.

As the attorney meeting proceeded at Legion & Associates, Roy sauntered out of the building. He first headed east on Broadway for ten blocks to Third Avenue and then headed north on Third Avenue for an uphill assent of six blocks to the corner of Third Avenue and Cedar Street. Situated on the northeast corner was California Western School of Law. Roy was slightly winded, but determined.

A voice then caused Roy to refocus.

"You got any extra change for a burrito?"

Roy looked in the direction of the voice and saw a homeless man with tattered clothes that appeared to be hundreds of years old and hair that looked like a fake wig because it was so matted and unkempt.

Roy just stared at the man and reached into his back pocket for his wallet. He retrieved the billfold and looked in it to find six dollars. He took the money out and handed it to the homeless man.

"God bless you," the homeless man responded.

"Wait," Roy said. He then reached into his pocket and pulled out thirty-eight cents in change. He extended his hand out to the homeless man who opened his palm and Roy dropped the change into it. Roy then continued on his journey.

He walked one-half block north on Third Avenue and the block passed over Interstate 5. Third Avenue created a bridge over the freeway that traveled north and south. This particular section was referred to as the downtown 'S' curve. Roy stopped and stared at the southbound traffic, which was moving at sixty to sixty-five miles an hour, as rush hour had concluded.

Roy looked up the street and then down the street. No traffic was coming and he saw no traffic in the distance. He stepped up onto the guard rails and grabbed on to a chain link fence that was in place to prevent pedestrians from jumping onto the freeway. Roy then tried to hoist himself up to climb over the fence with no success.

He then saw the homeless man, whom he gave money to, walking in his direction. When he was within ten feet, Roy called out to him.

"Hey, give me a boost."

The cacophony of sounds from the freeway made hearing difficult.

"I don't think that's a good idea," the homeless man stated.

"Please?" Roy uttered in desperation.

The homeless man jaunted toward Roy and began pushing Roy up at his butt, while Roy struggled to pull himself over the top of the fence. Within thirty seconds, he was over the top of the fence and holding on to the chain links for dear life.

Roy was rethinking his decision when he pictured Roger Legion in his mind. He let go of the fence and plummeted down to the freeway. The first thing his body struck was the hood and windshield of a tractor-trailer traveling at sixty-eight miles per hour. The windshield smashed and left a film of Roy's blood on it. Roy bounced off the truck and was struck and run over by four more cars before the traffic stopped. His head had been ripped off from his body.

Back on Third Avenue, the homeless man watched what happened from the overpass like a spectator at a sporting event. When it was over, he wanted to find a place where he could purchase a burrito.

CHAPTER 3

Roger Legion surveyed the attorneys in the conference room to make sure that he had their full attention before his weekly allocution began.

"Unibility Insurance is coming into our offices to conduct a legal audit of their files," Legion announced. "Most of you guys know what this is, but for the others – they will give us a list of files that they want to review. This is a legal audit, so they are reviewing the files to make sure the charges – what we have charged them – correspond with the work performed. Prior to their review, we conduct our own review."

It was then that Joe Frisch, a seasoned attorney, who had been at Legion & Associates for eleven years, and looked like he belonged on a magazine cover, spoke up.

"Roger, if we are firing on all cylinders here, doesn't this exercise seem to be duplicative?"

"Well Joe, I'd like to be able to say that I know what is going on with all the files, but I can't. The last thing I want is for outside lawyers to come in here and bring something stupid or negligent to my attention. We win at trial because we are prepared. So, let's be prepared for this little exercise."

As he finished his sentence, Roger noticed one of the attorneys yawning. Legion's eyes locked on to the yawner.

"Am I bothering you?" Roger asked.

"No," he answered, quickly and definitively.

Legion refocused on the group.

"If you handle Unibility files, you're off the hook for this exercise. I will have the list by the end of the day today. I will assign them on Monday."

"How much time will we have?" inquired one of the attorneys.

"I want it done by the end of next week, so we can go over any problems the following week. It won't be any more than one or two files to review."

Legion then pointed to another attorney, named Josh Stromsoe. He was thirty-eight years old, five feet ten inches tall, and weighed 185 pounds of what appeared to be solid muscle.

"Josh, you wanted to roundtable one of your files. We're all here. Go ahead."

"Well, it's more of a strategy discussion. We represent a bar in the Gaslamp District. Argument begins over a girl. Words are exchanged. A fight breaks out. When it's over, one of the patrons, not involved in the initial fight, is dead. It appears that one of the bouncers was overzealous and the owner told the bouncers to 'bust heads' if there was any trouble."

"When's the trial date?" Legion requested.

"Less than ninety days," Josh responded.

"Any settlement discussions?" Legion again posed his inquiry.

"No. Plaintiff wants big money. Seven, maybe eight figures." Josh was indicating that the plaintiff attorney was seeking a settlement that could exceed ten million dollars. "The insurance company doesn't want to pay anything near that amount of money, but the facts are terrible. I'm concerned that, at trial, it's going to be a train wreck."

"Gentlemen," Roger's baritone voice took control of the conversation. "At trial, you tell a story. A simple, convincing story. Every story has good facts and bad facts. How do you get rid of bad facts?"

He looked around the room and no one volunteered an answer.

"There are three ways: replacement, displacement, and misplacement. Steve," Legion randomly selected one of the attorneys, "how do you replace a fact?"

"You just put another fact in its place. Act like the original one does not exist."

"Tell your story without it," Legion relayed with definite certainty. "How do you displace a fact? Steve, you're on a hot streak, you might as well continue."

"You tell the story with that fact, but you minimize the importance of it," Steve shared.

"You take away its value. Remember, YOU are telling the story. YOU are in control. Finally, how do you misplace a fact?"

"You're going to have to help me with that one, Roger," Steve admitted.

"Think of your role in this instance like a magician. You have to focus the jury on where to look. What you do not want them looking at is anything that will sink your case. You have to come up with something more interesting and more compelling to capture their attention. It's all a game, but you can win it. If you do it correctly, there will be no end game. There will be no concession, there will be no surrender. All there will be is victory."

Roger stopped speaking to allow the concept to sink in.

"Let's do this, Josh. I will go over the file this weekend and let's discuss it Monday afternoon. If we have to, we'll go in and talk to the carrier. All right?"

Josh shook his head in acknowledgement.

"Okay, Brian," Legion declared and pointed him out at the table. "I need to talk to you in my office." He then turned his attention to the rest of the group.

"Gentlemen, let's sharpen our knives."

All of the attorneys rose from the table and exited the room. Brian Stensler followed Roger Legion to his office. Brian was average height, early 30s, and weighed 160 pounds. He was lanky and his clothes looked too large on him. He had curly, brown hair and wore braces.

Legion knew Brian was right behind him as they entered Legion's office. Roger walked directly to his desk and picked up a piece of paper off of the only pile of documents and turned to face Brian.

"What is this?" he asked with a serious tone and handed the piece of paper to Brian.

Brian looked at it and saw it was a Response to Interrogatories from one of his cases.

"Response to Interrogatories," he answered.

"What's wrong with it?" Legion's question demanded an answer.

Brian looked at it again and responded.

"There are no objections."

"Very good. You know we object to all interrogatories as being vague, ambiguous, and overbroad. Just in case we need it on appeal."

Roger stared at Brian with a stern visage.

"Should we get the paralegal up here?" Roger wondered.

"No, I'll take care of it," Brian told him with a reassuring manner.

"I looked on the billing sheet. I didn't find a charge for this," Roger told him, referring to the Interrogatory Response.

"I'll find out what's going on."

"Good. You have to keep a tight rein on these people."

"I will," Brian acknowledged with a smile.

"Let me know what the deal is."

Brian raced out of Legion's office and sprinted directly to the office of another attorney. Legion unknowingly stumbled onto something that was the tip of an iceberg.

CHAPTER 4

FBI Special Agents Robert 'Bob' Malloy and Peter 'Pete' Chrisman sat in their late model Chevrolet Malibu, parked on Broadway, heading west, within walking distance to the entrances of the America's Finest City Building. They were part of a stake-out team assigned to surveil a lawyer who worked within the building.

Pete Chrisman was forty-one years old, five feet eight inches tall, 210 pounds, with black hair combed over to the side. He wore a blue, pinstripe suit. Beneath his coat was a crisp, white shirt, with a checkerboard-pattern, blue tie.

Bob Malloy was thirty-seven years old, five feet ten inches tall, 180 pounds, with all of his head hair totally shaved off. He was African American and appeared to be in very good physical shape. He wore a black suit, with a light blue shirt, and a red tie with gold stripes.

"Is it almost time for a coffee run?" Bob asked not knowing whether or not Pete was listening.

Pete held up his Starbucks cup of coffee.

"You know this is a big waste of time, right?" Bob surmised. "Almost two weeks out here and we don't know what we're looking for."

"Hey, the assistant AG must know what she's doing, otherwise, they would have never okayed the manpower for this op." Pete was referring to the female assistant attorney general in charge of the operation that involved this stake-out.

"I could tell from the first day that we were briefed," Bob opined. "There is something personal going on here. I don't know what it is, but she's got an agenda. And you and I are going to be part of her game. Helping her hunt down a spook."

"Hey, I am racially offended by that comment," Pete told him with a raised eyebrow and smart-aleck grin.

"Okay, then you can call me 'honkey.'"

"Can we first find a time machine and go back to the 1980s?"

"What do you want to do about it then?" Bob requested a reply.

"How about we go to the town square and string you up? Like a lynching."

"I don't have any rope," Pete commented with deadpan seriousness.

Pete just looked forward. "Note to self, bring rope to work."

As if on cue, both men started to giggle and a quick rap was heard on the back-door, passenger window.

Bob unlocked the door and a woman entered the car quickly, sliding to the center of the back seat and leaning forward. She was thirty-seven years old, 123 pounds, five feet seven inches tall, and wore a Chic Pindot two-button, black jacket with matching straight leg pants. The woman also wore a white, button shirt that had the top button unbuttoned. She had blonde, shoulder-length hair and her makeup gave her face a flawless appearance.

She started to speak before the car door was even closed.

"Why are you parked in a loading zone?" she asked with her voice sounding incredulous by the situation.

"So, we can keep an eye on both entrances to the building," Bob explained, "and the entrance and exit to the parking garage."

"God damn it," she responded with vitriolic ire. "I could see you guys were a couple of dicks from a mile away. Maybe, we should just shrink wrap the car with the words 'Ferociously Blatant Idiots' on it or just put 'FBI.' What do you think Special Agents?"

"Daisy," Bob responded, trying to assuage her, "it might help if you tell us what you're looking for. We've been out here for nearly two weeks and this guy, Legion, is very punctual about when he gets here and when he leaves."

"Whoa, whoa, whoa, BOB! Let's not forget the pecking order around here. I do not want to become too familiar with the hired help. So, when you address me, it is 'Ms. Zacaro.' Understand? You and your boy are on a need-to-know basis. When I feel that you need to know something, I will tell you. Until then, you do what you're told. I command. You beg. I am investigating Roger Legion for his involvement in a criminal enterprise that involves mail and wire fraud. I need to know where he is and who he is talking to. Feel better now?" she asked with flailing sarcasm.

"When do you think you'll charge him?" Pete asked.

"When do you think you'll put a toe tag on Roger Legion?" Daisy retorted back immediately.

Pete just stared at her, not knowing how to respond.

"Where's the car?" she asked.

"Right where he parked it when he got here," Bob told her.

"How do you know that?"

"If the car moves, the tracker sends us a signal. There's no way we would lose the car."

"Legion would probably lose your tail going around the block. Where's the IT guy I told you about, Roy Sims?"

"We're not surveilling him," Pete immediately chimed in.

"Nobody is surveilling him now. They're scraping him up off the freeway. He just jumped off the Third Street overpass." She then let out an exasperated sigh. "I want daily reports on this. When I call, I want my calls answered immediately. If I catch anybody lying to me about where they are or where Legion is, you guys are going to be scrubbing toilets in Quantico."

Quantico is the location of the FBI Headquarters.

Daisy then slid across the seat, opened the passenger side door, and put one foot out of the car. She then stopped for one final comment.

"Just to give you guys the heads up, they're having a sale on Maxi Pads at Target. You guys probably need the one for heavy flow." Without missing a beat, she stepped out of the vehicle.

Daisy pivoted and bent down to look back in the open door.

"And move this goddamn car! Lazy pieces of . . ." She slammed the door closed before her finished sentence could be heard.

Bob and Pete watched her walk away, heading east on Broadway, away from the America's Finest City Building.

"Crazy Daisy. Should I shoot her?" Pete asked Bob in a calm and collected voice.

"Go ahead," Bob answered. "I'll say that I didn't see a thing."

CHAPTER 5

Roger Legion sat at his desk reviewing monthly hours billed to date by the attorneys and paralegals. He also compared them to the previous month and year. He performed this exercise on a regular basis looking for any anomalies or significant deviations from prior work. Whenever any abnormal activity was discovered, Roger immediately made it a point to have a sit down conversation with that individual.

His mahogany desk with burl inlay boasted authority. The contents on top of the desk were rather sparse: the law firm's landline telephone, his computer and his cell phone. Two of the walls of his office were floor-to-ceiling glass and the view from the twenty-fourth floor was like a living portrait that constantly changed throughout the day. The other walls were mahogany and covered with various photos and awards, testifying to a lifetime of success.

Legion removed a calculator from the top left-hand drawer of his desk and began working on a computation when his landline phone began to buzz.

"Yes," he answered.

"Keswick Thomkins is on line six," Nina, the receptionist, responded.

"Put him through," Roger quickly replied.

Keswick Thomkins or 'Kez' was a law school classmate of Rogers' who was now a general counsel for a company called Zukunft, located approximately 480 miles from San Diego in Palo Alto, California or Silicon Valley. This company specialized in providing software for remote, medical monitoring devices. These devices could provide readings for blood pressure, blood sugar, weight, and asthma to doctors in real time and then the doctor could make modifications to a treatment protocol without the need of the patient going into the doctor's office.

"Roger Legion," he answered, looking forward to the call.

"What are you up to my friend?" the voice blurted out.

"Just rowing the boat," Roger remarked with a smile. "I use to say, 'dancing in quicksand,' but then that became too realistic."

"Are you still slaying them in the courtroom?"

"Every chance I get," Legion uttered with certainty. "How have you been?"

"Personally, I've been good, but my company's got a problem and, in all honesty, I don't know what to do."

"Whatever you need, Kez. But my office is quite a ways from Silicon Valley."

"The problem is in your neck of the woods, Roger. Listen, I'm coming to town on Thursday. Are you available in the afternoon? Can I come in your office and talk about it?" Kez's voice echoed a plea.

Roger quickly reviewed his electronic calender.

"Sure. Three-thirty. If you're available, we'll go to dinner."

"I'd like that. I've got to get on a conference call. My secretary will call the day before to confirm."

"All right. It's always good to hear from you, Kez. I look forward to seeing you."

"Me too, Roger." With that the call ended.

Roger Legion had known Kez for more than forty years. He could tell from the tone of Kez's voice that the problem was more than just economic.

CHAPTER 6

Brian Stensler, the Legion attorney that Roger called into his office to discuss the errant Response to Interrogatories, raced to the office of Nedrick Chandler, a 205-pound former running back for the University of Arizona Wildcats, before being sidelined by damage to his Achilles tendon.

Brian entered the room like a meteor that would not stop until it crashed. Once he entered, he quickly returned to the door to close it. Ned looked up from the desk where he sat and placed a laser focus on Brian.

The two men stared at each other for a moment, wondering who should speak first. Ned started.

"What did he want?"

Brian handed Ned the Response to Interrogatories. Ned perused it and handed it back.

"Should I be worried?" Brian inquired.

"This is nothing. Don't worry about it." Ned responded, wanting to quickly quell his anxiety.

"Easy for you to say," Brian retorted. "What happens if he starts sniffing around the files? He starts looking through them. You and I have both been here long enough to know what happens to lawyers who try to cross Roger Legion. They're all listed on the Memorial Plaque out front."

"You and I," Ned said directly, "both went into this with our eyes open. Don't count on Legion to find anything. This," he said pointing to the Response to Interrogatories piece of paper, "was a coincidence. You remember why we got involved in our little enterprise?"

They stared at each other as Brian reflected. Then, Brian slowly nodded his head affirmatively.

"Tell me why?" Ned asked.

"We were tired of making Roger Legion rich. We wanted a 'bump.' A payday that would get us to a different place."

"Bingo!" Ned exclaimed. "Now, just go about the day like any other normal day. Remember, if anything happens to us, Legion goes down in flames with us. He won't let that happen."

"All right," Brian told him as a knock was heard at the office door.

Another lawyer stuck his head in and started to speak hurriedly.

"Hey, Ned. Roy Sims, the IT guy. They said he just jumped off the Third Street overpass onto the 5 freeway. Crazy, huh?" With that the attorney backed out of the office and closed the door.

Brian and Ned looked at each other in disbelief. As Brian thought about what he had just heard, the blood drained from his face. He renewed his inquiry to Ned.

"Should I be worried?"

CHAPTER 7

Night blanketed the city. Judge Harrison Ogilvie stood at the windowed wall of his twenty-eighth floor condominium in the Vivro Towers located just off Market Street in downtown San Diego and peered at the city looking east.

It was shortly after midnight and the Judge was restless. He had been a tennis player all his life and proud of the physique on his 71-year-old fit body. He had been divorced for the past fourteen years and none of his children lived in San Diego. Ogilvie traded in a successful law career for a position on the bench because he was tired of chasing clients.

His greatest joy from being a Judge came from giving out harsh sentences and watching guilty people grovel. The more they asked for leniency, the harsher the sentence he would impose. Any convicted individual who showed no interest in the time they were about to serve, had the greatest chance of getting a reduced or suspended sentence.

One of Judge Ogilvie's proclivities was a late night ride in his Lincoln Continental looking at what he deemed the 'living' dead. The 'living' dead were those that society gave no heed and were willing to do anything out of desperation and the need to exist. This was an activity that he was unable to do during the day.

The Judge decided that tonight, a ride was in order.

He took the elevator down to the lobby of the building and acknowledged the doorman on the way to the underground parking garage. His car emerged from the building with no pre-determined destination.

After spending only a few minutes downtown, he turned north onto Fifth Avenue and drove nearly three miles to Upas Street, where he made a right-hand turn. He crossed Sixth Avenue and entered Balboa Park.

While Balboa Park is known for the San Diego Zoo and museums, there are portions of it, at night that give way to criminal activity. The northern end of the park, where the Judge now drove, was dark and he continued to cautiously gaze for any movement.

The Continental pulled into a small parking lot off Balboa Drive that was shrouded by trees. There was a streetlight at the entrance to the lot, but it provided barely enough light to illuminate twenty-five percent of the lot.

Judge Ogilvie pulled into the lot and parked his car approximately halfway in. He kept the engine running and he saw a young man walk in front of the headlights approximately ten feet in front of the car. The man appeared to be in his late teens or early 20s weighing approximately 115 pounds, with zero body fat. His complexion was pale white. He wore pants that were skin tight on the legs and he wore a brown hoodie with a white, muscle t-shirt underneath. He had a moustache and his hair was perfectly coifed. He stopped at the driver's window of the Judge's car. The sound of the car's power window filled the air.

"Hey," the man said. "How's it going?"

The Judge just looked at him up and down before responding.

"Good."

"If you're looking to buy, I'm looking to sell," the man added in a weakened voice.

"What are you selling?" the Judge asked.

"Any fantasy you might have."

The Judge just stared at his face.

"How much?" Ogilvie asked.

"Can you do a hundred?"

"Get in," he told him with a nod of his head to the passenger door.

The young man hurried to the passenger side of the car and entered the vehicle. He positioned himself to get comfortable in the seat.

"Listen," the man said. "I got to make sure that you're good for the cash. Can I see it?"

The Judge reached into his pocket and pulled out a billfold. The outside bill was a one hundred dollar bill.

"All right," the young man told him. "Tell me what you want and where you want to do it."

"I know this hotel over in Point Loma," the Judge suggested. "They charge by the hour. I want to go over there."

"Lead the way, sweetheart."

While the man was speaking, a knock was suddenly heard on the driver's window. The car was surrounded by casual clothed policemen from the San Diego Vice Squad all with their guns drawn and aimed at Judge Harrison Ogilvie.

"Shut the car off!" one of them yelled.

Inside the car, the Judge turned the car off and looked over to his passenger.

"You're under arrest for solicitation of prostitution."

The Judge's door was opened, he was pulled out of the car, then pushed up against it to be placed in handcuffs.

As one of the officers read him his rights, Judge Ogilvie began working on a plan to do what he did best. Survive.

CHAPTER 8

At 2:55 am, in the San Diego County Central Jail located on Front Street in downtown San Diego, Judge Harrison Ogilvie sat in a small, sterile, crème-colored room with an aluminum table in the center, bolted to the floor and four stool-type aluminum chairs, also bolted to the floor.

Judge Ogilvie wore handcuffs and his handcuffs were locked to another chained restraint, attached to a metal ring that was soldered to the table. Judge Oglivie's hair was now disheveled and he wanted to use one of his hands to straighten it, but the handcuffs would not allow it. He stared around the room with an angry expression as if someone in his courtroom was about to be found in contempt.

The four walls of the room were half glass and he was able to see various people walking by the room. None of them noticed him. The Judge enjoyed being the center of attention in his courtroom, but here, he wanted to be invisible and kill everyone in the building for daring to infringe on his freedom.

It was then that he saw his lawyer, Wilson 'Buddy' Collins, a white-collar, defense attorney, whose reputation included the defense of former mayors, judges, city councilmen, and other high profile media defendants. He was tall and lean, mid-50s, and had a quirk of rolling his fingers. Some called it 'pill-rolling,' but Buddy claimed that it helped him to think. He had an Amish work ethic and was able to quote statutes by chapter and verse.

Buddy entered the room without much flare and closed the door behind him. He stood inside the doorway and looked at the Judge with a smile.

"Where have you been?" the Judge demanded, finding no humor in his smile. "I called you two hours ago."

"Sorry, your honor, I sleep at night," Buddy answered throwing a yellow pad onto the table. "What happened? They tell me you're being very disruptive."

"It bothers this fine police community, because I know my rights. Now, I need your help to make this disappear."

"What do you mean – disappear?" Buddy quizzed.

"You got your cell phone?" the Judge asked.

"Yeah," Buddy answered, gazing down at him as he stood there.

"I want you to call Marsha Crawford. She's a secretary at the U.S. Attorneys' office. Get the number for an attorney named Daisy Zacaro. She's the Chief Attorney for the General Crimes Division. Tell her I'm down here and I want to talk to her about Roger Legion."

Daisy Zacaro was the attorney who berated the two FBI special agents who were surveilling Roger Legion. They had given her the moniker, 'Crazy Daisy.'

"Why don't you let me bail you out? We'll say you were entrapped and the police were just overzealous." Buddy believed his solution would appeal to the Judge's common sense.

The Judge looked at Buddy with a furrowed brow and a cold, sober visage.

"Solicitation of prostitution is a crime of moral turpitude. The DA is going to report me to the State Bar. Just for engaging in it, I could lose my job and be disbarred. Entrapment as a defense is not going to help me. Now, I told you, we are going to make it disappear. You understand?"

Moral turpitude is a legal concept that refers to conduct that is contrary to community standards and good morals. Judges and lawyers may lose their license to practice law if they engage in such behavior.

Buddy retrieved a pen from his coat pocket and jotted down a telephone number from the Judge. He then left the room and headed back to the front desk where his cell phone was being held.

Judge Ogilvie sat in solitude preparing a presentation for Crazy Daisy.

CHAPTER 9

Four hours earlier, Federal Attorney Daisy Zacaro sat in the living room of her Carmel Del Mar, California condominium wearing only a white bathrobe and panties. She was perched at the end of her emerald-green, leather couch with her legs tucked under as she sipped a glass of Beringer White Merlot. She gazed at the appointments within the room and her thoughts were interrupted by the doorbell.

She rose and made a hasty jaunt to the door. She opened it and there stood a man, who upon first impression appeared to belong in a biker gang. He was over six feet tall, in his late 30s, wore jeans, a black t-shirt and a jean vest. He had full sleeve tattoos on both arms, mostly naked girls, dragons, and demons. He wore thick, black rimmed glasses and his face was heavily scarred from childhood acne. He carried what looked like a large doctor's bag.

"Get in here," Daisy told him before he could say a word. He entered and looked around.

"Where we gonna do this?" he asked in a deep, baritone voice.

"The bedroom," she replied. "This way."

He followed her into the master bedroom and a single, white sheet had been placed on top of the bed. The man set his bag down and began removing items. The first thing he removed was an aluminum tray and placed a pre-cut piece of non-stick wax paper on it. He then took a straight-edge razor, a disposable scalpel, and latex gloves from the bag. He placed the items on the wax paper that sat in the aluminum tray.

"You got shaving cream?" he inquired.

"Yeah, it's on the counter in the bathroom," she responded in a rather, brusque tone.

"You gonna get ready?" he queried.

She stared him directly in the eye and undid the belt on her bathrobe, dropping it to the floor. Then, she slid her panties down her legs and kicked them off. She showed no sign of discomfort or embarrassment with being naked in front of this man. Daisy then lay down on top of the sheet and pushed away a pillow that was near her head.

The man then removed two sets of handcuffs from his bag and connected one to each of her wrists and then to the headboard of the bed. He then proceeded to obtain leg shackles from the bag and restrained her legs to the footboard of the bed, making sure that her legs were spread.

The final item he removed from the bag looked like a small set of jumper cables that were attached with an eighteen-inch, small chain. "You want these?" he asked.

"Yes," she replied without doubt.

The last item that he pulled from the bag were nipple clamps. He attached each end to the nipple of her B-cup breasts. Then, he proceeded to the bathroom and washed his hands. After drying them, the man emerged with a can of shaving cream. The final preparation was the donning of the latex gloves.

The man proceeded to lather up Daisy's pubic area and used the straight-edge razor to shave it clean. After the man cleaned the razor, he removed the disposable scalpel from its plastic container. All the while, not a word was spoken between either of them.

"You want a towel to bite down on?" he asked while preparing for the next stage.

"No," Daisy answered as if perturbed by the question.

"Is there a safe word?" he wondered.

"Harder," she answered without thought. "If there's no blood, you're not doing it right."

"You should let me do a tattoo," he urged. "It'll hurt once and that's it."

"I'm not paying for your opinion, I'm paying for your talent."

"You're the boss," he said in a dismissive tone and focused on her pubic area.

"Don't forget it," Daisy decried like it was a mandate.

The man then began his procedure. He had done it several times before today. In Daisy's pubic area that he had just shaved, the man used the scalpel and began to carve a word into her.

CHAPTER 10

As dusk turned to dawn on this Saturday morning, Judge Harrison Ogilvie sat stoically in the attorney/client conference room of the San Diego County Central Jail awaiting the arrival of United States Assistant Attorney General Daisy Zacaro. During the entire evening, he took one bathroom break and had no interest in small talk with his attorney, Buddy Collins.

His jailers were allowing the Judge special dispensation to wait in this room longer than generally allowed. The Judge's harsh sentencing made him a favorite in law enforcement circles.

As Buddy checked his watch for the sixth time, the door sprung open and Daisy Zacaro entered like a conquering force landing on a beachhead. She wore a black double-breasted DKNY trench coat over a Nordstrom gingham cotton dress.

Her crotch still burned in the area where she allowed her visitor, hours earlier, to cut her. She relished the pain. The area that was shaved was now covered by a large non-stick adhesive first-aid pad.

As she entered, Daisy took a visual scan of the room and began to speak immediately.

"I hear someone has been very busy," she stated in a devious tone.

"Miss Zacaro, I'm Judge Harrison Ogilvie and this is my attorney, Buddy Collins."

"I sorta figured that out," she answered with a wry smirk.

"Pleased to meet you," Buddy added as an afterthought.

"Why don't you tell me why you need to bother me on a late Friday night – slash – early Saturday morning?" Daisy inquired with bitter disdain for the Judge.

"Would you care to sit down?" Buddy asked.

"I'll stand," she responded immediately, primarily due to the pain of her recent bondage procedure. "Now, what do you have for me, Harry?"

"My client," Buddy began, "would like to make an arrangement with you that in exchange for certain information you would have all the charges for the," he hesitated for a moment, "current situation dismissed."

"Not dismissed," the Judge adamantly announced. "I don't want any record that an arrest ever occurred."

"We believe these charges have no merit to begin with. The Judge was obviously entrapped," Buddy began what promised to be a persuasive legal argument when he was cut off by the Judge.

"Cut the bullshit, Buddy." He then directed his gaze to Daisy. "You came to talk, Daisy. Let's talk. Everybody in this town knows that you have a hard-on for Roger Legion. You want Roger Legion?" The Judge paused for a quick moment. "I can get him for you. I just have to do it my way."

"Enlighten me on how you can get him?" her voice dripped with disbelief.

"Are you familiar with the mediation service, Vici Resolutions? It's one of the largest mediation and arbitration

44

companies in the western United States. And it's owned by Roger Legion. Several times removed, of course, through various shell corporations. He's got a daughter, who's a stay-at-home mom. She's also a lawyer and the CEO of that company."

"All I've heard so far is that he's a rich prick. Now if that was against the law, I think you would have been in here a long time ago, Harry." She knew that he preferred the name, Harrison, but enjoyed his squirming.

"The mediators at Vici Resolutions are all former Judges," Ogilvie explained. "He pays them in a month what they used to make in a year. That's the sweet plum that everybody on the bench wants. And Roger Legion decides who gets it. So, nobody says no to Roger Legion. He gets what he wants."

"So, you think you can get him to bribe you?" she asked with dripping sarcasm.

"I know I can. If he likes you, he takes care of you. Cars, or deals on cars, country club memberships, he'll help you get a mortgage at a smoking low-rate."

"Bribing a state judge is not a federal crime," Daisy conceded. "But maybe he's got a few federal ones in his pocket. Are you going to wear a wire?"

"Yes," the Judge answered without pause.

"How long do you think it will take?"

"By the end of next week," he again swiftly answered.

Daisy looked at the Judge and ruminated.

"I will talk to the District Attorney. I think we can do business. But let me warn you, Harry. You may think that you know me, but let me assure you that the one thing I specialize in is vengeance. If you don't live up to your part of the agreement, I promise you that I will bring the wrath of God down upon you and you will curse the day that you called me."

As she finished, she turned to grab the door handle. The Judge's lawyer, Buddy, spoke up.

"Do we need anything in writing?" he inquired.

"I don't," Daisy said turning back to them. "I had my tape recorder going the entire time." As she spoke, she removed a small, handheld voice recorder from her pocket and showed the men. A Cheshire cat smile filled her face.

She again started to leave, but stopped and turned around again.

"Harry, I was just wondering. Why didn't you call Roger Legion for this instead of me?" She was referring to his recent interaction with the law.

"I had a problem once before that he got me out of. He said he wouldn't do it again."

"Like I said when I walked in, someone has been very busy." She then reached for the door handle and exited the room.

Judge Harrison Ogilvie and his attorney, Buddy Collins, stared at each other for a moment.

"No comment," Buddy said in disgust.

CHAPTER 11

On the following Tuesday, at 3:35 pm, one of the twenty-fourth floor elevators of the America's Finest City Building opened and off stepped Keswick 'Kez' Thomkins. This was the man who was Roger Legion's classmate at California Western School of Law and also was the general counsel for a remote, medical monitoring company called Zukunft, located in Palo Alto, California.

Kez Thomkins was tall, solid, and weighed approximately 250 pounds. He had a full head of gray hair, wore tortoise shell glasses, and an impeccably tailored Brioni, blue suit.

The reception area of Legion & Associates was awash in marble and leather. The floor was black marble with a center inlaid design of a lion's head. The sofas were made of brown, Italian buffalo leather. The cushions regained their shape as soon as a visitor stood. The receptionist was a petite, young lady named Nina who wore a Calvin Klein petite floral print A-line dress. Her hair was blonde and shoulder length. Her makeup flawlessly accented her China doll complexion.

Behind the raised, granite countertop, where Nina sat, in large letters proclaimed the words, 'Legion & Associates.'

"Can I help you?" Nina asked with sweet, smiling charm.

"I'm here to see Roger Legion. I have an appointment."

"Can I get your name?"

"Kez Thomkins."

Nina proceeded to push two buttons on her telephone pad.

"Kez Thomkins is here to see you." She waited a moment. "Sure." She then turned to her visitor. "You can go into the conference room," she said pointing to the western side of the building. "Would you like something to drink?"

"I'll take a water if you have one," Kez acknowledged.

"Right away," Nina said as she quickly rose from her chair.

As Nina scurried to the kitchen to obtain a bottle of water, Roger Legion made his way to the large conference room. When he entered, both men had smiles that beamed.

"It's been too long, my brother," Kez proclaimed and met Roger Legion with a hug. They stepped back and looked at each other. "When did you get so old?"

"Shortly after you did," Roger answered with a smile. "Let's sit. You want something to drink?"

"The girl is getting me a water," Kez replied as he rolled a chair back from the table and sat. Roger followed suit.

"How's Shirley and the kids?" Roger asked.

"Well, they're all working on bankrupting me and shortening my life exponentially," Kez answered with a grin. "How's Val and your kids?"

"They're doing well. Everybody's healthy. Knock on wood." As he spoke the last sentence, Roger rapped his knuckles on the table."

"You keeping busy?" Kez wondered.

"Always. You?"

"I find that the more money I make, the less I have to do. My life as a general counsel is either a kiddie pool or a tsunami. Not much in between. I've come to see you today about a tsunami."

As he finished the sentence, Nina entered with a bottle of water and a glass filled with ice. She set it down in front of Kez.

"Would you like something to drink, Mr. Legion?" she asked.

"No, thank you, Nina. I'm fine," Roger responded.

She smiled and left the room. Kez opened the water bottle, poured a glass, and began to speak.

"My company is the target of an extortion plot and I don't know what to do. I was contacted by an attorney down here in San Diego, named Rike Hessler, who claims that he has a client who has photographs for sale of our CEO, a guy named Kurt Liesel, engaging in various sex acts and bondage with children."

Kez looked out the window for a moment and shook his head.

"Is it true?" Legion asked with deadpanned enthusiasm.

"I don't know," Kez answered with a tone of surrender. "I asked him and he unequivocally denies it. He's forty-eight years old, never married, and I've never seen him with a woman. Although if you go out with him, he talks about girls like a drunken sailor. He goes to Germany about every six weeks and he always talks about all these deals he's got going on over there. But in the nine years that our company has been around, we have never received a penny from Germany."

"If he denies it, how does he explain the photos?" Legion wondered.

"That's where the story gets a little hazy. My marching orders are to pay this guy, Rike, for the photos."

Legion looked at him and shook his head.

"To me, that's a blatant admission of guilt."

"He has his reasons. Our company, Zunkunft, is scheduled to have an initial public offering of its stock within the next 120 days. The CEO and I are the two largest shareholders in the company. If the stock goes out at Wall Street's valuation, he and I will both be worth in excess of $250 million. We have suppliers and customers in the Midwest who would run for cover if they knew our CEO was involved with child pornography. These are the reasons he wants it paid."

"So, what do you want me to do?" Legion asked. "Get the guy arrested? Chisel the guy on the price?"

"No. My concern is how do we know once we pay him that he did not make a copy of the photos and they won't turn up again? Essentially, I want you to consummate the deal and make sure the proper legal safeguards are in place, so once we pay this guy, he is out of our life."

"That could be tough," Roger conceded.

"That's why I came to you," Kez admitted. "I knew that you would know how to handle it. I would like to tell this attorney, Hessler, that you are representing us and he should contact you to make arrangements for a meeting to discuss this matter."

"All right."

"Another thing. I would like to send two million dollars down to you and label it as a retainer. The company really wants to distance itself from this matter. I would also ask that only you handle it. The fewer people who know about it the better."

"That's no problem."

"Good," Kez commented as a smile returned to his face. Now, can you direct me to your bathroom? My kidneys have been working overtime."

"I'll show you."

Both men stood and exited the room. In the reception area, Roger directed Kez to the men's room. As he finished, Nina called out for his attention.

"Mr. Legion, there is a man on the phone who says he must talk to you and it is urgent. He says his name is Doc."

Nina's message stopped Legion and brought him concern. He quickly moved to Nina's raised granite countertop and motioned for the telephone receiver. She handed it to him and connected the call."

"Hello," Roger answered cautiously.

"Ten-ten Second Avenue. Eighth floor conference room. Twenty minutes. Go now." Then the caller disconnected.

Legion slowly handed the receiver back to Nina as the wheels in his mind began to smoke.

Legion knew from the tone of the voice that the problems this day were about to get worse.

CHAPTER 12

Brian Stensler, the Legion attorney with whom Roger Legion discussed an errant Response to Interrogatories, quickly rapped on the door of fellow attorney Ned Chandler as he entered.

"What's up?" Ned asked deflecting from his perusal of an online court docket.

"What do you think is going to happen with that audit?" Brian wondered.

"Nothing. Who cares?" Ned replied dismissively as Brian took a seat across the desk from him. "It's not our problem. We don't work on Unibility Insurance files. We're done with our little project. There's no way it can be traced back to us."

"I hope you're right," Brian replied, not all that certain of Ned's comment. "Did you ever hear anything about Roy?"

Roy Sims was in charge of intellectual technology at the firm. He committed suicide six days earlier by falling onto the Interstate 5 freeway from an overpass.

"He's ancient history," Ned proclaimed. "He's already been forgotten."

"I don't know about forgotten," Brian stated as he rubbed the side of his mouth. "I can't wait for these braces to come off."

"How much longer do you have them on?"

"About six weeks."

"Listen, I heard something today, but you've got to keep your mouth shut," Ned's voice lowered as he spoke.

"What?" Brian inquired with serious calm.

"Five attorneys are thinking about bailing on this place and either going to another firm or starting their own shop," Ned uttered the fact with slight glee. "If that happens, it will decimate this place."

"I wonder if they're thinking about taking any files with them?" Brian speculated. "Because if they are, they should look at the Memorial Plaque and ask Paul Clifford's ghost."

Paul Clifford was an attorney who worked at Legion & Associates for more than twelve years and then decided to open his own law firm. Five years earlier, he planned to take the files that he was working on with him to his new firm. Two days after he told Roger Legion of his intentions, he was in a car accident that killed his wife and two children. Paul believed that Roger was involved in causing the accident.

Paul became despondent, his mental health was eroding, and his life was spiraling out of control when one day he decided to exact revenge on Roger Legion. It occurred on the same day that a firefight erupted in the large conference room at Legion and Associates. Paul saved Roger Legion's life that day before he was shot to death.

"If those guys hit the road, this law firm is not going to last. This could give us the perfect cover," Ned observed.

"I'll believe it when I see it," Brian expressed with doubt. "I don't think you or those guys know the reach of Roger Legion. I hope that our third wheel has taken that into consideration."

"I spoke to him last night. He's got an airtight plan to move the money. Once it's safe, we split it up," Ned disclosed.

"Three ways, right?"

"Three ways."

CHAPTER 13

The skyscraper located at 1010 Second Avenue was once the tallest building in the city. Built in 1963, it was twenty-five stories high and contained nearly 325,000 square feet of office space. More than twenty years earlier, Roger Legion had his office in this building.

After saying goodbye to Keswick Thomkins, and discussing plans to pick him up later for dinner, Roger Legion left the office and moved at a brisk clip down Broadway for eight blocks to the 1010 Second Avenue building. He was followed closely by FBI Special Agent Bob Malloy who was one of the two agents assigned to surveil Legion. The other agent, Pete Chrisman, followed both of the men in an FBI unmarked Chevrolet Malibu.

Legion entered the building and Agent Chrisman was less than ten feet behind him. They both entered the same elevator and Chrisman saw that Legion pushed the button for the eighth floor.

"What floor?" Legion asked him.

"Eight," he responded, looking at Roger Legion right in the eye.

When the elevator stopped at the eighth floor, Chrisman realized that there was only one tenant on that floor, a law firm called Nash & Bigelow. Their specialty was estate planning.

Legion entered the main door to their office and held the door for Chrisman to enter. Knowing he had no business in there, he came up with a quick excuse.

"I'm going to the men's room first," he told Legion and Legion let the door swing closed.

Chrisman moved down the hallway in an attempt to watch the door from an obscured location.

Inside the office, Legion proceeded directly to the receptionist. Before she could say a word, Roger began to speak.

"I'm Roger Legion," then the girl cut him off.

"He's waiting for you in there," she advised, pointing to their conference room. Roger made a beeline to the door and entered posthaste.

Inside the room, pacing at the far end near the conference room table was retired Superior Court Justice Joseph Webb. He was seventy-six years old, a little man, straight out of central casting with balding, white hair, glasses, and a slight arch in his back. At one time, he was a mentor to Roger Legion and taught him many tricks of the courtroom arena. Roger came up with the nickname of 'Doc' for him because he could take any situation and improve it.

Doc stopped pacing when he saw Roger and both men stared at each other for a quick second. Roger spoke first.

"What's with all the cloak and dagger?" Roger's voice demanded a response.

"You've got to help me," Doc answered with meted desperation. "The FBI came to talk to me today. They were asking me about my mortgage. They wanted to know how I qualified for one after that bankruptcy three years ago. They had questions about Vici Resolutions."

Vici Resolutions was a mediation service surreptitiously owned by Roger Legion. The FBI was made aware of this after Judge Harrison Ogilvie was arrested for solicitation of prostitution and thereafter cut a deal with the Assistant Attorney General, Daisy Zacaro.

"What did you tell them?"

"Nothing. I said I couldn't remember."

"All right. I'll find out what it is," Legion assured him.

"Listen, Roger," Doc spoke as if he was about to disclose to Legion that he had a fatal disease. "It's something big. The reason we're over here is because the phones are tapped in your office and the FBI have you under surveillance."

"Bullshit," Roger declared, repulsed at the notion.

"I called around. The warrants were sealed and they got a Federal judge up in Orange County to sign them. This thing's got something to do with mail and wire fraud. You got guys coming into your office to look at files in the near future?"

"Yeah," Roger acknowledged referring to the insurance company audit set with Unibility Insurance.

"They're going to be undercover FBI guys. This must have something to do with the guy from your place who jumped from the bridge."

Legion's anger placed him deep in thought for a moment and quickly continued with his questions.

"Who's behind this?"

"There's this new skirt in the attorney general's office. Her name is Daisy Zacaro. Word is she hates your guts. And she's pulling out all the stops."

"Do you know why?" Legion queried.

"No. But I have nothing to do with insurance files, so I don't know why they're turning up the heat on me."

"They're just trying to roust you. See what they can get out of you. Don't worry about anything. Keep your mouth shut." Legion ordered.

"What if they come to talk to me again?" Doc speculated.

"Tell them you want a lawyer," Legion answered definitively.

Doc looked down to the ground and tapped the top of one of the conference room chairs.

"I've come too far, Roger. I'm not going to throw it all away over foolishness."

"Don't worry, Doc. I'll find out why Miss Zacaro's got a problem and why the FBI is so interested in me."

"Be careful, Roger. They knew too much about Vici Resolutions. They must have gotten to somebody on the inside."

"I'll find out," Roger assured him. "Keep your ears open. I'll contact you tomorrow with a secure number to call me on. Thanks, Doc."

"You want to thank me, make this thing go away."

Roger Legion despised the thought of being a pawn in someone else's game, either at his law firm or by the FBI. It was time for heads to roll.

CHAPTER 14

The Office of the United States Attorney for the Southern District of California was located at 880 Front Street, which was on the corner of Front and Broadway. This building formerly housed the Federal Courthouse until a new Federal Courthouse was built next door to it in 2012.

Shortly after Roger Legion returned to his office after visiting with Doc, the retired Superior Court Judge who shared with Roger details regarding the FBIs investigation of Legion & Associates, Special Agents Bob Malloy and Pete Chrisman were summoned by United States Attorney Daisy Zacaro to her office. When they entered, she was looking down at her desk.

Daisy looked at both of the Agents and her visage brewed with anger. The men stood across the desk from her and remained silent.

"Where did Legion go?" she spoke fast with a cold, detached tone.

"Ten-ten Second Avenue, the eighth floor," Pete Chrisman, who followed Legion on foot, answered the questions as quickly as they were asked.

"Where on the eighth floor?"

"It was a law firm, Nash and Bigelow."

"Who did he go see?"

"I didn't follow him inside," Pete replied.

"What did you do while he was inside?" Daisy's gaze was locked on to Bob.

"I waited for him."

"How long was he in there?"

"About thirty minutes."

"Who is Doc?" Daisy asked the question as if she had just caught him in a lie.

"I don't know."

"Why do I know who Legion went to see and you don't?"

Bob gave his shoulders a quick shrug.

"We didn't have that intel," Bob responded.

"Did you ever think about calling the telephone surveillance unit to see if they knew who Legion was going to see? Because they DID!"

"As soon as he came out of the building, I started to follow him on foot and Special Agent Malloy followed close by in the car," Pete replied in defense of his actions.

"Can you do two things at once? Like walk and talk on a telephone?" She then turned to Bob Malloy. "Or drive and talk on a telephone?"

"With all candor, ma'am that is against the law in California." Bob knew as soon as he finished the sentence that he should have never said it.

"SHUT UP! Are you being a smartass, boy?" She spoke as if she was about to lunge across her desk and rip his throat open. "How about I make a phone call and get you transferred to some godforsaken arctic tundra outpost in Alaska? Dealing with Eskimos being attacked by polar bears on Federal property. They don't give you a car over there, they give you a snowmobile. After being here in paradise, I bet you wouldn't like that? I can make it happen. And I know, watermelon and fried chicken are tough to come by over there," she uttered with a sly smile focused on Bob Malloy. Pete Chrisman stood with his mouth open and could not believe her racial comment.

She then picked up a stack of their daily reports and dropped them to the desk.

"This shit is useless," Daisy retorted in disgust. "The surveillance is over. You are both still assigned to assist in this investigation. First thing in the morning, I want you to go to the Loma National Bank branch in Calexico, California and pick up the original signature cards for the Copyization account."

She then picked up a Manila envelope and handed it to Bob.

"Here's the subpoena. Why do you think they opened the account in Calexico?" asking as if it was a trick question.

"I would assume there is no video surveillance at that branch," Pete suggested.

"Perhaps, you're not as worthless as I've been led to believe. I still have a grave concern about the competency of both of you men. Never forget: I command, you beg. Now, get out of my sight!"

Both men left Daisy's office and did not start to speak until the doors of the elevator they entered began to close.

"You think I could take her in a fight?" Pete asked nonchalantly and then gave a sly look to Bob.

"No," Bob answered without thought. "Maybe if I helped you."

"What kind of help would you give me?" Pete asked.

"I'd shoot her."

"Word," Pete answered definitively and put his fist out to bump Bob's fist.

Part 2

CHAPTER 15

SANDPOINT, IDAHO
6 WEEKS EARLIER

Sandpoint, Idaho is located in the northern panhandle of the state, less than fifty miles south of the Canadian border. It is the largest city in Bonner County, with a population of slightly less than 7,400 people. It lies on the shores of Idaho's largest lake, the forty-three mile long, Lake Pend Oreille and is surrounded by three mountain ranges (the Selkirk, Cabinet and Bitterroot). It is the home of Schweitzer Mountain Resort, the State's largest ski resort. It was once deemed the "Most Beautiful Small Town" by Rand McNally and USA Today newspaper.

Inside Monarch Mountain Coffee, located on Fourth Avenue in Sandpoint, three blocks from Lake Pend Oreille, a man sat in the corner of the establishment at a small, round table, with one leg crossed over the other, awaiting a visitor. The man was impeccably dressed, perhaps to a metrosexual level, wearing a tailor-made gray suit, with a light blue pinstripe running through it. Instead of a tie, he wore a purple and gray, stripe silk cravat woven ascot with a matching pocket square handkerchief and a white shirt. His shoes were Barker Black Ostrich Cap Toes. This particular pair costs nine hundred seventy-five dollars.

The man was sixty-five years old, five feet eleven inches tall, with a slender build. He had a full head of white hair and wore wireless-rimmed glasses.

He gently sipped on his "Shot in the Dark" expresso awaiting a visitor. It was mid-afternoon and the foot traffic in the coffee shop was exceptionally light. His corner table was surrounded by two additional chairs. The wall behind him was completely covered by a large mural of a nighttime scene of the buildings along the waterfront.

The man was mid-sip when he heard his name called out.

"Dash?"

"Yes," he responded, quickly wiping his mouth and standing to attention. "Mr. Lorin?"

"That's me," he answered with a smile and exchanging a handshake.

"Please sit," Dash suggested with a hint of a French accent, while motioning to one of the chairs. "May I call you George?"

"Absolutely," he responded.

George Lorin appeared to be in his late 50s or early 60s with white hair and a white moustache. He was approximately six feet tall and lanky, with a firm, yet sturdy frame. He wore jeans with a herringbone sport coat and a blue, button shirt.

"Let me get the introductions out of the way. My name is Henri Charlemagne. I am a French Canadian. I have dual citizenship. By occupation, I am a haberdasher – a maker of fine men's suits. Thus, my nickname – Dash." He stopped for a moment and looked around. "Let's get you something to drink."

Dash caught the attention of an employee and called her over.

"George, tell this young lady what you would like to drink. I recommend the 'Shot in the Dark' expresso. It's the first thing that I think about when I wake up in the morning."

"Just a regular coffee," George responded.

"Cream and sugar?" the waitress asked.

"Yes, please."

The waitress walked away and Dash began speaking immediately.

"They wait on their regular customers at the table. I don't like those coffee places where you stand in line. It reminds me of a soup kitchen."

The waitress returned with a coffee and set it down in front of George.

"Put it on my tab," Dash advised. He then turned his attention to George.

"My father's family opened the first fur trading post, just north of here in the early 1800s. It was the first non-indigenous settlement in the Idaho Territory. They say Lewis and Clark stopped there on their way to the Pacific Ocean."

"Interesting," George acknowledged with a nod.

"I share this with you so that you understand me a little better. My family was hit hard by the depression. We were 'piss poor.' You know what that means?"

George shook his head in a negative fashion.

"Poor families would collect their urine and sell it every day to the local tannery, who used it to tan the animal skins. The tannery paid two cents a day. At the end of the week, you got a dime."

"That sounds pretty tough," George admitted.

"My father was a taxidermist," Dash continued. "But his real gift was tracking pelts – fox, mink, chinchilla. You have to skin them properly in order for them to be used in creating a fine garment."

"I didn't think animal fur would be very popular these days," George interjected.

"Fools do not understand that since the dawn of time man has used animals as protection to keep warm. They are perfect for that purpose. I am a person who is not intimidated by anyone, especially a fool."

"Are you still making suits?" George asked.

"Of course. Only the finest. Although, it's difficult to compete with Hong Kong these days. I take pride in my creations. I personally place every stitch. A machine never touches any garment that I produce. This suit I'm wearing," Dash answered waiving his hand up and down in front of the suit. "The fabric on this suit is Italian wool and cashmere, gray with light blue pinstripe woven suiting. Italy produces the best fabric. Egypt had quality fabric at one time, but not anymore. May I?"

George had no idea what Dash was requesting, but Dash put out his hand to George's lapel and placed two fingers behind it and rubbed his thumb along the outside of it.

"Olivine/white herringbone wool tweed. A middle of the line product. Brooks Brothers?" Dash quizzed.

"Very good," George retorted. He was impressed.

"I want you to understand that I am very detail oriented. And I am always well researched. Now, let's talk about you."

The haberdasher had placed his cards on the table. It was now time for George Lorin to tell his story.

CHAPTER 16

At 5:15 am, the next morning, Roger Legion sat at Nina's desk in the reception area of Legion & Associates waiting for a visitor. He admired the cleanliness of Nina's work area and he recalled when he designed the lobby and reception area of the law firm. He wanted the visitor to realize that they were entering a place where war was planned, strategy devised, and the execution of a plan commenced. The reception area was to demand awe of the visitor.

A bell was heard announcing the arrival of an elevator. The doors opened and a tall, thin man, in his early 40s, stepped off wearing a worn t-shirt, jeans, and work boots. He wore a tool belt and carried a tool box. His final accoutrement was an extremely worn baseball cap that had a San Diego Chargers logo on it.

The man looked around quickly and spotted Roger.

"Are you Mr. Legion?" he asked.

"Yeah," Roger replied as he stood from Nina's chair.

"I'm Fred from the phone company. Rolf sent me. You think you got somebody listening in?"

"Yeah," Roger shared.

"All right. Do each of the offices have their own line or do they all pour through your receptionist?" Fred wondered.

"They all come through the receptionist," Roger replied.

"Okay. I'm familiar with the layout of this building. I'm going to go check the telephone panels and I'll be right back."

Fred then called an elevator for travel to the first floor of the parking structure to review the telephone maintenance area of the building.

Roger returned to his office and approximately thirty minutes later, Fred returned. He found Roger in his office.

"They have been listening, but it's not the normal FBI setup. They either pulled it or they're listening to you sporadically. What I did was make line twenty-four on your phone a secure line. It'll be safe for you to talk on that one. I also put an amplification device on your lines. If you start to hear scratching, they're listening. Get off the line and call them back on line twenty-four."

"Very good."

"I also put a pin camera in down there. I'll get an alert if somebody touches the lines. We'll also get a video of them." Fred smiled at Roger. "We good?"

"What do I owe you?" Roger posed his inquiry as he reached for his money clip.

"No, it's all right. Rolf said I can't take any money," Fred was adamant.

"You married?" Roger asked.

"Yeah," Fred answered nodding his head affirmatively.

"Take your wife out to dinner," Roger told him as he peeled three one-hundred dollar bills from his money clip.

"Happy wife, happy life, right?" Fred shared and Roger smiled. Fred picked up the bills and put them in his pocket. "Let me sweep your office for any bugs. I got the stuff here."

Fred entered Roger's office and began to assemble a wand-like device used to detect the minutest listening devices, especially

those used by the FBI. This was the beginning of house cleaning at
Legion & Associates.

CHAPTER 17

George Lorin was taking a long sip of coffee as Dash was changing the conversation to George's backstory. He set his cup on the table and leaned back in his chair.

"I've lived all over the central part of the United States," George confessed, "never hanging around anywhere for too long. I try to stay clean and I try to stay off the grid. I don't have a Social Security number and I've never paid taxes. My father was always afraid that I would get drafted and he didn't want me to have any part of it."

"No wife? No kids?" Dash wondered.

"Could never find one who would put up with me. I enjoy being a vagabond. A hobo," George shared.

"I don't know too many vagabonds wearing Brooks Brothers clothing."

"I've done rather well for myself as an independent contractor."

"That's my understanding," Dash conveyed. "If our mutual friend, Rusty, wasn't invited by the Idaho Department of Corrections to spend the next fifteen to thirty years in the Maximum

Security Institute down in Boise, I would be having this conversation with him right now."

"Rusty's a good man. But I think he was getting greedy. And one of his crew flipped on him," George said.

George was telling Dash that one of Rusty's confederates decided to testify against him and assist the police.

"How do you know Rusty? He recommends you highly," Dash quizzed.

"I literally met him at a bus station. I sold him a car I was trying to dump. He asked me if I would be his wheel man for a smash and grab outside of Seattle. A jewelry store. It was a couple of hours and he paid me thirty grand."

"Rusty tells me you have nerves of steel," Dash told him with a smile.

"I do what is necessary to get the job done."

"That's what I like to hear," Dash asserted. "George, I'm a man of opportunity. I don't believe in luck. You have to make your own luck. But when opportunity raises its head, you must seize it and capitalize on it. I realized a long time ago that I could never retire from simply making suits. So, I decided to invest in opportunities."

"Dash, I also consider myself a man of opportunity. But the payoff has to be worth the effort."

A smile filled Dash's face.

"Mr. Lorin, let's talk business."

CHAPTER 18

Judge Harrison Ogilvie's courtroom was located in Department 61 of the Hall of Justice. This building, situated at 330 Broadway, was only four blocks from the America's Finest City Building. It housed the Superior Court's Civil Independent Calendar Courts. These were the courts visited by the attorneys at Legion & Associates on a very regular basis.

The interior of the courtroom was spartan, yet efficient. The walls were a crème color and all the chairs, including the jury chairs, had the seats and backs covered in a navy blue cloth. The wood was a Brazilian Cherry with clean lines around the Judge's bench and the court clerk's desk, located directly next to it.

On this day, there were no trials going on in this department and the day's Motion Calendar was rather light. This was done by the design of Judge Ogilvie. Since the day he was arrested for solicitation of prostitution, he could think of nothing but the agreement he made with US Attorney Daisy Zacaro. He agreed to provide her with information that would implicate Roger Legion in a scheme, whereby judges would be given a position at a mediation company called Vici Resolutions. This was in exchange for favorable treatment by the judges, while they were still on the bench.

On today's calendar, in Judge Ogilvie's department, attorney Brian Stensler brought a motion to continue a trial date for thirty days to accommodate his client's hernia surgery. The plaintiff attorney in the case said that they would not oppose the continuation, so this type of motion would normally receive perfunctory approval.

Brian Stensler arrived at the appointed time, 10:25 am for a 10:30 am motion time and he checked in with the court clerk. She was an older woman, who seemed to be interested in Brian's face and his business card, because she would alternate back and forth, looking at both of them. Brian was slightly taken aback by the light foot traffic. Judge Ogilvie was famous for his 'cattle calls' where he would have a packed morning session and handle any overflow or unresolved issues in the afternoon.

Brian's dental braces continued to annoy him as they would either cut his tongue or the inside of his cheek. A lowly associate from the plaintiff's firm arrived that Brian did not recognize. As soon as Brian sat down, the bailiff announced that court was in session and Judge Ogilvie assumed his perch on the bench.

He looked at the top sheet of a pleading and then lowered his reading glasses to his desktop.

"What's the first case?" the Judge asked the court clerk.

"*Mackenzie versus Fleming*," the court clerk declared. The few attendees and the attorneys moved from the gallery to the courtroom area. Each man took a seat at a table facing the Judge.

"Mr. Stensler, I believe this is your motion. Am I correct?" The Judge's voice had no emotion.

"Yes, your honor," Brian answered as he stood.

"What seems to be the problem here?" the Judge asked speaking slow, as if parsing his words.

"My client is scheduled to have a hernia operation two days before the trial is set to begin and he needs a little time to recuperate."

"But the operation will be over, won't it?"

"Yes," Brian answered cautiously wondering where the Judge was going with this line of questioning.

"I don't see why he can't be here. He's only going to sit in a chair. Are you going to call him as a witness?"

"That decision hasn't been made yet," Brian advised.

"Who's making that decision?"

"I may. I am not sure yet," Brian continued to wonder about the reason for these questions.

"You don't know much about this case, young man. You going to try it?" the Judge asked leaning forward in his seat.

"Possibly," he replied. "And I'm very knowledgeable about this case."

The Judge brought his left hand up to his mouth and pulled it down his face.

"Am I sensing some attitude? I don't appreciate it." The Judge's grimace was evolving from sheer anger. "Son, we both know that if this trial sees the inside of a courtroom, it's going to be tried by Roger Legion. Why isn't he here today?"

"He had another engagement," Brian answered, fabricating his response on the fly.

"So, it's okay to disrespect me for somebody else?"

"Your honor, no one is disrespecting you. This is a rather simple motion and you're complicating it. Now, you want to grant it or deny it?" Brian quizzed with conviction.

"I want to sanction you five hundred and one dollars for your conduct and attitude in my courtroom."

Brian was incredulous. He could not believe the Judge would order a sanction over something so foolish. The State Bar of California requires any sanction in excess of five hundred dollars be reported to the State Bar. The sanction would become a part of Brian's public record.

Judge Ogilvie then stood from his chair and picked up the pleading that sat in front of him. He shot a final parting glance at Brian.

"Get Legion down here now!" He then retreated to his chambers.

The plaintiff attorney walked over to Brian.

"What the hell was that?" he asked.

Brian gazed forward and then turned his head to the other attorney.

"Madness."

CHAPTER 19

George eagerly anticipated Dash's so-called opportunity. Dash made a quick scan of the room before beginning.

"To provide you with full disclosure, the two men sitting in the far corner of the room work for me."

George looked over his left shoulder and saw the two men. One was a younger man in his mid-30s, with black glasses that had wire rims on the bottom of the lenses. He wore a white shirt and brown tie. He was balding and appeared to be a nerdish bookworm.

The other man wore a large Stetson cowboy hat and his face was craggy and weathered by the sun. He wore jeans with a denim shirt and cowboy boots that had silver inlaid toe tips.

"The man without the hat is Pierre. He is, how do you say, my right-hand man. The other fellow is Tex. He is my . . . muscle."

"Why does a haberdasher need muscle?" George wondered.

"Even an Avon lady needs muscle. It just makes things move along more – smoothly."

"I understand."

"Good. Do you have any experience with armored trucks?" Dash queried.

"None per se. I met a guy once who was a manager at an Albertsons, the grocery store, in Billings, Montana. He told me the routine for the armored car pickups. I got a Loomis Fargo uniform, walked in, and they handed me the cash. I did it three times in one hour before they even knew they were robbed. I cleared nearly $125 thousand without a gun."

"Most impressive," Dash shared. "What I have is access to the trip tickets for an armored truck company called Parapet Logistics, out of Boise. The Friday before Labor Day is one of their biggest hauls of the year. Summer's over, children going back to school, and stores want to get rid of their excess inventories of cash."

Armored truck trip tickets provided the location and time for a particular pickup along a truck's route. They are highly secure and not published until the day of the pickup.

"What do you estimate the takedown to be?" George asked.

"Minimum $3.5 million. Could be over $5 million."

"You've got my attention," George shared.

"Good," Dash acknowledged. "One of the routes that day is referred to as the Mondo Run. It has several banks, Walmart, Target, and grocery stores. It starts in Boise and comes up here to Sandpoint. The one thing that I also have is the location of the last pickup of the day. It's the Gemstone National Bank on East Superior Street near First Avenue. Right by the entrance to Highway 95. I figure you make your move after that."

"Seeing as you have access to the trip tickets, you obviously have an inside man. Do you think I could get one of my men on the armored truck crew?"

"Not enough time," Dash answered with certainty. "The inside man is one of the owners. Apparently, the armored truck business is not as profitable as he desires. He has insurance and his share of the take comes out of my cut."

"Are we talking fifty-fifty?" George asked.

"That's my desire. I have the information and you're doing the heavy lifting."

"What are your plans after you get your hands on the cash?" George asked.

"I have a banker that I use in Miami," Dash expressed. "All we have to do is get it to him and he takes the risk of loss from there. He moves it offshore and then cuts us a legitimate check, complete with a ten ninety-nine form, so we can pay our taxes like good, honest citizens."

"What does he charge?"

"Seven and a-half percent."

"What's his name?"

"Angelo Troy."

"I'm going to want to talk to him."

"Perhaps, we can set up one of those calls through the computer," Dash conveyed. "Let me ask you: Do your people all have clean records?"

"Yes," George answered emphatically.

"I expected nothing less. The last thing you want is for one of your crew to be picked up the night before a job for a parole violation."

"I'm gonna need some seed money," George asserted.

"Of course," Dash acknowledged. "How much do you think?"

"One hundred thousand dollars," George answered without hesitation.

Dash then snapped his fingers to call out to his right-hand man, Pierre.

"Pierre. *Viens ici, maintenant!* (Come here, now!)" Dash then turned his attention back to George. "English is not his first language, so some things need explanation."

Pierre arrived at the table and Dash whispered into his ear. Pierre scurried out of the building.

"You will have it shortly," Dash explained. "I can also assist you with any technology or weaponry that you may desire."

"I appreciate the offer, but I have my own people that I use."

"Understood."

"There is probably some additional information that I am going to need from your inside guy."

"I will give you Pierre's phone number. You call him anytime and tell him what you need. For something like this, we use disposable phones. I will make sure he tells you when he will be changing the phone and to make sure that you get the new number."

George could not think of any more questions at that moment.

"How long you been making suits?" George inquired.

"I have been assembling ensembles for over forty years." Dash shared.

George then noticed what appeared to be a cane, leaning against the wall that had a large, clear Lucite diamond, slightly smaller than a baseball, on the top of it.

"Is that your cane?" George wondered.

"It's not a cane. It's a walking stick. A fine accoutrement to any man's wardrobe."

George stared at Dash for a moment wondering what his love of fine clothing was really masking.

CHAPTER 20

Roger Legion entered Department 61 within twenty-two minutes after receiving a phone call from Legion attorney, Brian Stensler, detailing the events that took place at the motion hearing. Roger wore a gray suit, with a tie that was stripped in red, blue, and gray. He also wore gold cufflinks with a Mother of Pearl stone attached to each one. He carried nothing in his hands.

Legion initially made his way to Brian and the plaintiff attorney, who were sitting next to each other. The plaintiff attorney gave Roger his version of the events, which corroborated Brian's rendition.

Roger then made his way to the court clerk, but not before speaking with the bailiff.

"Hello, Bobby," Legion exclaimed as he walked up to him with a firm handshake greeting. The bailiff rose from his chair to meet him.

"How you doing, Mr. Legion?" he acknowledged with a wide smile.

"I'm keeping busy. How about you?"

"They got me bouncing around. I'm picking up extra shifts wherever I can."

"You still go up to North County?" Roger wondered.

"Yeah. I prefer that courthouse. I live up there."

"Bobby, it's always a pleasure," Roger concluded with a wide grin.

"Same with me, Mr. Legion."

One of Roger's skills was the ability to communicate with anyone and not talk down to them, unless he wanted to talk down to them. He would always portray a genuine interest in the person speaking to him.

Legion proceeded to the court clerk and stood at her desk facing her. She looked up. He did not introduce himself, but she knew who he was.

"I'll tell him you're here," she advised and immediately trekked back to his chambers.

Judge Harrison Ogilvie emerged from his chambers in less than a minute and stood in the doorway between the courtroom and the outer area of his office, where his secretary would sit.

"I am going to talk to each side, regarding this motion," the Judge announced. "I'll start with the defense. Mr. Legion, you come in. Just you."

The Judge looked off in the distance to Brian Stensler and gave him a slight snarl.

Roger followed the Judge to his chambers and the Judge closed the door after Roger entered. The office was large, approximately thirty by twenty feet, mahogany walls, decorated with plaques and awards. There was also the clichéd bookshelf filled with *California Reporters* that no one ever read.

The Judge took a seat at his large, oak desk and offered a chair to Roger. He refused.

"How have you been, Roger?" the Judge asked in somewhat of a magnanimous style.

"Fine," he answered in a perturbed tone.

"How's work?"

"You're not very good at small talk," Roger opined.

"You're right," the Judge confessed. "Most times, when I'm talking to somebody, I think in my head, why am I talking to this guy. I can't stand this piece of shit."

"Your honesty is refreshing. Now what am I doing down here?"

"Your boy out there has an attitude. And I don't like it. These kids today have to learn respect."

"Well, let me ask you this, *Your Honor*," Roger said with percolating anger. "How many sanctions have you ever handed out and, in particular, how many have you handed out at a motion to change a trial date?"

"Listen," the Judge replied and waved his hand in the direction of the courtroom. "Forget that bullshit. You can have your trial date moved. But we need to talk."

"What do you want to talk about?" Legion's response indicated he did not have much interest in anything the Judge was about to say.

"Vici Resolutions. I need that gig. I need you to wave your magic wand and make it happen. Come on. Do this for me," he pled. "We'll go out in the courtroom. I'll make everything right. Just like I always do for you."

"Your honor," Legion began with an iron snarl and piercing steel-blue eyes focused on the Judge's eyes. "I have no idea what you're talking about. I don't make decisions for Vici Resolutions. And if you are trying to imply any impropriety on my part in your courtroom or any courtroom, then I take umbrage at that accusation. Now, do you want to discuss the case at hand, or not?"

"You, Roger, are truly an asshole," the Judge concluded.

"Don't worry about the motion to continue the trial. My client will be here. We are going to bring a motion to recuse you from hearing this case based on your animosity toward my lawyer and me. Don't worry about the sanction. If you sign an order for it, we're going to appeal it. I'll also file a complaint with the Commission on Judicial Performance in regard to your attempt to bribe me just now."

"And what proof would you have?" Judge Ogilvie snidely asked.

"Let's say you were either wearing a wire or had a recording device operating right now," Legion calmly suggested. "I could use that."

The Judge stared at him and slowly began to shake his head in a negative manner.

"Mr. Legion, you and your law firm are like a kite in a tornado. There are forces out there that are working day and night on your eradication. I could help you, but you're too blind to see."

Legion turned and walked to the door. He grabbed the handle and turned back to Judge Ogilvie one last time.

"Hey, Harry. How was the ride in the police car Friday night? Good times?" Then he exited as the Judge continued to stare at the door.

Roger knew that the Judge would never issue the sanction against Legion attorney, Brian Stensler. The Judge did issue an order to extend the trial date an additional forty-five days. Legion never filed the Motion to Recuse the Judge because he knew the case would settle prior to the trial date.

Legion was bothered about the Judge's comment regarding forces trying to eradicate him and his law firm. He wondered if he was referring to the FBI or someone else.

CHAPTER 21

After saying goodbye to George Lorin, Dash finished his expresso drink and thought about his next move. Both Pierre and Tex watched him and awaited his command.

"Get the car," he barked from across the room and both men moved into action.

Dash stood and made sure that his coat, shirt and ascot were perfectly positioned before he began to move. He reached for his walking stick and began a slow, pronounced saunter out of the building. Tex pulled up near the entrance in a white, late model Mercedes-Benz S550, with crème interior. As Dash approached, Pierre stepped out of the passenger door and opened the back passenger-side door for Dash's entry. Dash stepped into the vehicle and Pierre closed his door.

"What do you think?" Pierre inquired through a thick, French accent.

Dash stared out the window as if in deep thought.

"Something about him bothers me," Dash shared. "Tex, make sure one of your men keeps an eye on him. But for the most part, he's perfect." Dash then changed his tone. "Pierre, call our

man at Parapet Logistics. Tell him, we need to have a meeting."
Then a moment passed. "Did the new fabric bolts come in?"

"They should be at the warehouse now."

"*Allons-y!* (Let's go!)" Dash ordered and Tex began a non-stop journey to the home of Dash's empire, Henri's Haberdashery.

CHAPTER 22

Roger Legion sat at his desk the next morning and scanned a list of files that was recently provided to him by Unibility Insurance. These were the files selected for the legal audit. Roger's friend, Doc, told him that the audit would be conducted by undercover FBI agents.

Legion forwarded the list to his personal secretary, Louise, and asked for the files to be brought to him. Roger wanted any files that were on the twenty-third floor brought to him immediately. If any files were in the attorney offices, they could be brought to him at a later time.

Roger then pulled up another screen on his computer and scrutinized the law firm's billings for the Unibility account to determine if any appeared to be excessive. All of the totals fell within an average range that was normally charged to the Unibility account. Based on the law firm's accounting records, nothing seemed out of the ordinary.

It was then that he was struck with an idea. Legion picked up the receiver from his office telephone and pressed two numbers. His secretary, Louise, answered.

"Yes, Roger?" she asked.

"I want to look at Roy Sims' email. Can you tell me how to do that?"

"Let me get his Username and Password and I'll call you back," she said.

As he was returning the receiver to its cradle, his phone rang.

"Yes," he responded.

"Kez Thomkins is on line six," Nina, the receptionist, shared with him.

"Put him through," Roger answered.

The phone rang again and Roger pushed a button to answer the call.

"Hello, Kez," Roger declared in an exuberant voice.

Kez Thomkins was the law school classmate of Roger's who was now the General Counsel for a company called Zunkunft. The CEO of that company was being blackmailed by someone claiming to have photographs showing the CEO involved in child pornography. Roger was asked to assist in paying off the blackmailer, even though the CEO denied the allegations.

"Hey, Roger. Just touching base to see if you made contact with that lawyer."

As Kez spoke, a scratchy sound could be heard on the line. Roger had the phone lines checked to see if they were tapped and a scratchy sound indicated someone was listening.

"Let me call you back," he quickly responded and ended the call. He then called Kez on line twenty-four, the secure line installed by Roger's contact at the phone company. Kez answered immediately.

"Hi, Roger," Kez declared.

"I spoke to Mr. Rike Hessler and I am meeting with him tomorrow afternoon at my office.

"Okay. Sounds good. Let me know what happens."

"I will," Roger told him and with that the call ended.

Roger was perturbed that the FBI was listening in on a call with a client. Unless the call relates to the specific activity which they are investigating, they would have to get off the call immediately. Kez and his company were extremely concerned about keeping the matter quiet.

Legion made a decision at that moment that he would not sit by idly and be slapped around by the FBI or anyone. He rose from his desk and began a march down the hallway to the elevator. He advised Nina that he would be back. His destination was the Office of the United States Attorney for the Southern District of California.

It was time to take off the boxing gloves and put on brass knuckles.

CHAPTER 23

As soon as George left the coffee house, he proceeded to the Gemstone National Bank, the one selected for the last pickup on that Friday before Labor Day, and began to study the layout of the parking lot. The bank was situated at the end of a small strip shopping center that had no major anchor store. In front of the bank was a large parking area with fifteen cars in each row and the rows were situated perpendicular to the bank in two-by-two columns.

On his second day of reconnaissance, he saw a Parapet Logistics truck enter the parking lot for a delivery to the bank. Two men exited the truck and only one entered the bank. What George found more interesting was the action taken by the driver while the two other employees made sure their delivery safely reached its destination.

When he was not at the bank, George went to the Sandpoint Library, located on Cedar Street. He utilized their computer and books for research on armored trucks.

On the Friday of that week, George decided it was time to start making phone calls. His first phone call was to Dash's right-hand man, Pierre.

"Pierre, it's George."

"'Ello, George," he answered, dropping the 'H.'

"Is it safe for me to tell you on this line what I need?"

"Yes. Go ahead."

"I need to know the type of truck, make and model," George conveyed. "I also need the radio frequencies. The final thing I want is some background information on the crew."

"All right," Pierre replied. "Give me a few days. Can you come by the warehouse next Wednesday, say two o'clock?"

"I'll be there."

"Very good."

With that the call ended. The next call was to an old friend of George's, named Mose. He was a rather non-assuming fellow who lived in Tekoa, Washington, near the Idaho border. He had an exclusive clientele and was a supplier of the most sophisticated weaponry and technology in the Northwestern United States.

To contact Mose, you had to first leave a message at his mother-in-law's house indicating who you were and when you wanted to speak to him. Mose called George shortly after receiving his message.

"Hey, George-gee, how are ya?" Mose asked emphatically as soon as George answered.

"I'm good, Mose. How 'bout you? You keeping busy?"

"You know, a little a this and a little of that."

"Good to hear," George told him. "Listen. I'm planning a fishing trip. You got any rods and reels I could use?"

"Sure," Mose responded. "How's next week? On Friday. I gotta bring my kids to school in the morning, but I should be in the clear after nine o'clock."

"I'll be there, Mose."

"I'll see you then, George-gee."

The final call was to an acquaintance named Anthony Smith, who went by the moniker, 'Smitty." He was a sniper in the first Gulf War and had extraordinary talent with weapons. When he was not on a job, he worked at a car wash in Butte, Montana.

"Hey, Smitty," George declared as soon as he answered.

"*Que pasa* (What's up), my brother?"

"What's the name of that steakhouse you used to talk about in Coeur d'Alene?"

"The Wolf Lodge."

"I want to check it out. You interested?" George requested, more like a commanding officer than a friend.

"I'm always interested," Smitty replied.

"Good," George confirmed. "Find a date that's good for you in the next week. I want you to bring Floyd, Gar, and Rollo with you. Let me know the day and time."

"Ten-four," Smitty declared. "I'll be in touch."

The wheels of the plan were continuing to turn without impediment. George was always concerned when things were going too smoothly.

CHAPTER 24

Earlier that morning, Assistant US Attorney, Daisy Zacaro, gave a weekly briefing on the status of various major cases currently headed for trial or in development. The meeting was videotaped, as always, to provide continuity in the event the lead attorney was unable to proceed with it. It also provided a record of who was in the attendance in the event any information leaked out.

Daisy was in charge of the Major Frauds Section in the office. Her unit dealt with complex investigations and trials involving all types of financial fraud, including money laundering and forfeiture cases.

Also in attendance at this meeting was Terrance Haden, the United States Attorney for the region. He had been recently appointed by the President and was Daisy's boss.

Daisy wore a Tahari ASL Four-button Crepe Skirt Suit with ivory copper Easy Spirit Raphael Pumps. She had a Power Point presentation for the group. The first slide said 'LEGION & ASSOCIATES."

"The activity here," Daisy began, "is quite simple. Any third party billing at Legion & Associates that exceeds five hundred dollars is sent directly to the insurance company for payment. So, if a Legion lawyer receives a bill from a copy service or any expert witness that exceeds five hundred dollars, they merely pass it along. It's a common practice at most law firms."

The next slide read "Manufactured Invoices."

"Unibility Insurance noticed an uptick in vendor billings being handled by Legion & Associates. This uptick was traced back to one particular vendor, called Copyization. The bills did not receive much oversight from the claim handlers at Unibility because they were authorized by either a Legion attorney or Legion himself."

"Any chance the authorization was forged?" Terry Haden, the US Attorney asked.

"It's a possibility," Daisy told him, "But this activity appears to be so widespread, it is definitely the result of more than one attorney."

"How many instances?" the US Attorney again inquired.

"It could be as high as two hundred," Daisy advised. "We should know exactly once we complete an audit of the files at Legion's office. Some of the charges may be legitimate."

"What's the dollar amount?" she was asked.

"Unibility believes it may be as high as three-quarters of a million dollars."

"That does not seem to be that much money to take such a risk," the US Attorney concluded.

"I believe it was a test run. To see if he could get away with it. Legion could then pull the same scam on all his other insurance companies."

"What's your plan after the audit?" another attendee asked.

"We'll quantify the fabrications and charge him with that many counts of wire and mail fraud, in addition to conspiracy. I also want to charge him with racketeering under the RICO statute."

The RICO statute, or the Racketeering Influenced and Corrupt Organizations Act, is a United States Federal law that provides for extended criminal penalties and a civil cause of action for acts performed as part of an ongoing criminal investigation.

There was a knock at the door and the receptionist for the office opened the door slightly and waved to Daisy.

"We're not to be disturbed, Ellen," Daisy barked with a strident voice.

"There's a man here named Roger Legion and he's demanding to see you," the receptionist uttered.

The attendees at the meeting looked at each other in disbelief that the subject of their meeting, Roger Legion, was waiting in their reception area.

An evil, vicious smile took over Daisy's face. She immediately walked out of the meeting and directly to the reception area for a head-on collision with Roger Legion.

CHAPTER 25

The distance from Monarch Mountain Coffee, the place where George first met Dash, to Dash's office, Henri's Haberdashery, was only one and a-half miles. The office was located in the thirteen hundred block of North Division Street, a commercial district, and the travel time was five minutes.

The office was a two-story, concrete block structure, which did not have much signage. The front of the building had a faux brick veneer. The interior of the building was less than ten thousand square feet. There was parking on three sides of the building and the next closest structure was approximately one-half mile away.

George approached the front door on this Wednesday as he had promised Pierre. The two glass doors were locked, but a doorbell was available to announce visitors. There was also a security camera to observe the visitor before a decision was made to grant or deny entrance.

Pierre arrived at the door swiftly, unlocking it to allow George's entry and then re-locking it.

"George. Welcome. Any trouble finding the place?" Pierre wondered with his thick, French accent.

"No," George responded. "This town is pretty easy to get around."

"Let me give you a little tour. Dash is on the phone. He will join us shortly. He may duplicate some of the things that I am going to tell you."

"That's fine," George responded with a nod and a smile.

"Very good," Pierre commented as they walked throughout the first floor. "On the first floor is where all the manual labor is performed. We have a room for coats, a room for trousers, a room for suitcoats, and a fourth room for miscellaneous items. Dash oversees it all and probably does ninety percent of the work himself."

George observed each room and was impressed by the cleanliness and the order of items and tools.

"In the center of this floor," Pierre shared, "we have a measuring room and a refrigerator room. The refrigerator room is where we stock our furs, both as pelts and as a finished product."

As they circled around the floor, George noticed a glass display case, approximately six feet high that contained a mannequin wearing a green suit, with a vest, that had light threads of white and red that were hardly noticeable until you looked closely at the garment.

"What's the story with this?" George inquired.

From behind George came a raised voice.

"The story is," Dash began, "that suit was made for a man named Louis Stephen St. Laurent, a former Prime Minister of Canada. If you look closely at the fabric, it contains very light white and red stripes woven into the green fabric. Red and white are the colors of the Canadian flag."

George turned to look at Dash, who wore a blue silk suit, perfectly tailored, with a white shirt and a yellow cravat with a red, diamond pattern.

"I don't say this often, Dash," George conveyed. "But you look good."

"Dupioni Italian silk," Dash told him. He then waved George closer to him to feel the lapel of the coat. "Feel it. Silk can be very slippery and difficult to work with. What you see here is a work of art. Only the best tailors are capable of creating such a piece."

"I guess you're in that club," George told him.

"What do we have for our friend, George, today, Pierre?"

"Give me a moment and I'll get it."

"How are your plans coming along?" Dash inquired.

"It's coming along. I should have everything in place within the next week. Then, it's just rehearsal."

Pierre returned from his office. He handed George a manila envelope.

"The radio codes are in there," Pierre disclosed. "As for the type of truck, there are two different trucks that they would send that day. Our man doesn't want to insist on a particular one. The details are in there on both of the trucks."

"Are they newer trucks?" George wondered.

"No," Pierre answered. One is a 2007 and the other is a 2004."

"Okay. What about the crew?"

Dash answered this question.

"He supplied us with their job applications and any disciplinary problems. There's not much, but it's in there."

"I guess I'm set," George concluded.

"Do you want to try to put in a call to my money guy, Angelo Troy?" Dash asked.

"I checked him out, he seems legit," George replied. "How long have you been doing business with him?"

"Seven years."

"I don't need to talk to him. But I don't know yet if I'm going to send my money to him."

"I understand," Dash told him. "Come upstairs and we'll finish the tour."

The three men walked over to the elevator and Dash called it, even though the stairs were available to walk up the one flight.

"Can I ask you a question, George?" Dash quizzed.

"Sure."

"How old are you?"

"How old do I look?"

"Tough to tell with the white hair," Dash told him. "You've got the skin of a young guy."

"I'm fifty-eight."

"A very young looking fifty-eight."

George smiled, but he feared a crack in his plan. The dam had just sprung a pinhole leak. It had to be plugged before the dam burst.

George would not be derailed. As a courtesy, he continued his viewing of Henri's Haberdashery. But his focus was on work to be done.

CHAPTER 26

In less than twenty minutes, Roger Legion was on an elevator heading to the third floor and Room 6923, the San Diego office of the United States Department of Justice. Before entering the office, he was required to walk through a metal detector. Roger's cufflinks and belt buckle set off the detector, but one of the Department of Justice uniformed officers passed a wand detector over him and allowed him to proceed.

Legion walked directly to the receptionist and stood in front of her until she gave him her attention. She was a heavyset woman with poorly applied makeup.

"I'm here to see Daisy Zacaro. My name is Roger Legion."

"Do you have an appointment?" she asked.

"No. Tell her I'm here. She'll see me."

Legion's voice was strident and demanding. The receptionist was intimidated. Knowing that Daisy was in a meeting, she rose from her chair and walked back to their conference room.

Within two minutes, Daisy approached. Her face projected enmity, antagonism, and resentment. Roger turned to her and his face showed an angry chagrin. When Daisy was within ten feet of him, she started to speak.

"What do you want?" she said in a dismissive tone.

Legion matched her voice with impatience and ire.

"I want to know why the telephones in my office are tapped. I want to know why I'm under surveillance. And I want to know why you have such animus toward me!"

"It's funny. I was just in a meeting and your name came up. I hope you understand that I'm unable to comment on an ongoing investigation. So, why don't you go back to your office and preach your gospel. Tell your little lawyer boys what a bitch I am because I won't kiss your ass. Go tell them, 'Gather around, look children, where I took a crap.' They look at it and tell you how great it is and how they love the fragrance, because their daddy never hugged them or told them that he loved them. You poison their minds and they follow you to their deaths. That's why I have such animus toward you."

"If you're looking for a fight," Legion assured her, "I can oblige you. But you have to ask yourself: Is this the fight I want?"

"I'll tell you this. I will not rest until I see you in an orange jumpsuit. Officer," she called over toward the door, snapped her fingers, and got the attention of one of the uniformed officers. He walked over to her at a quick clip. "Escort him off the property. If he refuses, arrest him for obstruction and trespassing. If he resists, shoot him."

Legion stared at her in disgust.

"Let's go," the officer said to Legion in a low voice.

If Daisy was a man, Roger would have considered a right hook to her face in a physical attempt to show Daisy the type of fight she was undertaking. Legion understood now how dangerous she was because she was driven by blind emotion. That type of adversary will do anything, legal or illegal, to achieve their goal.

CHAPTER 27

The town of Tokea, Washington sits just west of the Idaho border in an area of rolling hills referred to as the Palouse. This is a major agricultural region that primarily produces wheat and legumes.

Tokea has a population of approximately eight hundred people and retains a small town charm. It's rare to see outsiders and most people enjoy life in anonymity.

On the outskirts of town, just off Seamon Road, George Lorin drove down a dirt driveway and parked in front of what appeared to be a dilapidated barn. The patina of the barn was weather-worn. It appeared as if it had not been painted for well over fifty years.

"Hey, George-gee!" a voice from behind him exclaimed, calling his attention.

George turned and there he saw a 280-pound man, wearing a t-shirt, shorts, and flip-flops. He had black hair and three days of beard growth. He also wore a big, infectious smile.

"Mose," George proclaimed, returning the enthusiasm. "You old son-of-a-gun! How are you?"

The men met with a quick hug and stepped back to look at each other. Mose pointed to his own hair and then to George's moustache.

"What's this bullshit?" Mose asked.

"It's necessary for what I've got to do," George advised.

"Well, how you been? Good?"

"Yeah. Good. What about you?"

"I'm trying to lose some weight, but it's hard. You know. I like the carbs too much."

"How's the family?" George wondered.

"Everybody's good. My kids are getting big."

"How old now?"

"My daughter is ten and my son is seven," Mose proudly proclaimed. "My wife is still at the hospital. You know, as a nurse."

"That's great."

"So, you ready to do a little shopping?" Mose asked.

"Lead the way."

George followed Mose into the barn after Mose undid a padlock to allow entry. The aged patina of the building was part of the design of the building. Inside, the building sat on a steel frame with a high ceiling and a concrete floor. Mose walked over to a circuit-breaker box and tripped two of the circuits.

One of the concrete panels, approximately fifteen by fifteen feet, rose from the floor to display an elevator. Mose touched two different fingers on a biometric display next to the elevator doors. The doors opened and parallel lines of light ran down from the top of the elevator door to the floor. Mose turned to George.

"Check this out."

Mose entered the elevator, followed closely by George. Inside the elevator, the door closed, and the buttons for the three lower floors had a green backlight to them.

"If you had any kind of electronic device on you, the backlight would be red and we would not be going anywhere. Take your keys out."

George proceeded to remove his keys from his pants pocket. Mose then used a biometric eye scanner and before the scan was complete, the keys were wrenched from George's hand to the ceiling, where they appeared stuck to it.

"They call me the magnet man. If you pulled a gun on me, I'm able to activate a magnet using the eye scan," George shared.

"Very cool. I hear Glock's got a plastic gun," George commented.

"The shells of the bullets are still made of metal. We tested it. Come on. We'll go down to the showroom."

Mose once again allowed his eye to be scanned and the elevator began to lower one floor to the first of three floors. Mose was a purveyor of all things necessary to commit a crime. Weaponry, explosives, communications, and transportation were all available at a price. Mose was also into fabrication of anything special to assist the criminal in achieving their goal.

The two other floors of Mose's underground shopping center consisted of the second floor, devoted to research and development, and the third floor, the lowest floor, devoted to warehousing and an underground vehicle garage. There was no portion of the floors that was not under video surveillance.

They stepped off the elevator onto the first floor. It had a very clean, warehouse feel. It was similar to a Costco warehouse store, only smaller in size.

"So, what do you got going, George-gee?" Mose wondered.

"Armored truck," George replied.

A devilish smile came over Mose's face as he nodded affirmatively.

"Let me show you what I got."

CHAPTER 28

At Legion & Associates, Ned Chandler raced into Brian Stensler's office and stared at Brian while he finished a phone call. Ned appeared anxious and this caused Brian to accelerate the conclusion of his call.

"I'll check the dates with my guy and get back to you." He paused for a moment. "Okay, take it easy." Brian hung up the phone and turned his attention to Ned. "What's up?"

"We need to talk about the movement of certain stuff. What are you doing after work?" Ned spoke in somewhat of a hushed voice.

"Nothing. You want me to come to your place?" Brian wondered.

"No," Ned told him. "Let's go to a public place. How about Ruby's at the Mission Valley Mall? Six-thirty?"

"Okay. But what are you so nervous about? Is anything wrong?" Brian asked.

"I heard a rumor that the telephones here are tapped. No more talking about our little adventure on the phone. Understood?"

"Should I be worried?" Brian demanded a response.

"No," Ned assured him. "I told you. Stick to the plan. It's almost over. We'll discuss it tonight."

"Ned, I am not going to throw away everything for this. You remember, it started as a dare just to see if we could do it and I think it's getting out of control."

"Take it easy. Stay cool and everything will be all right. I'll see you tonight at six-thirty."

Ned fled the room and Brian stared out the window without focus fearing for his job, his law license, but most of all, fearing Roger Legion.

CHAPTER 29

George and Mose walked down one of the aisles of his underground criminal provisions store as their conversation continued.

"The Friday before Labor Day," George shared, "up in Sandpoint."

"You gonna take down the Mondo Run?" Mose wondered.

"That's the plan."

"Nice," Mose replied approvingly. "You going to take over the truck while it's stopped or do you want to stop it?"

"The plan is to take it over while it's stopped, but I want to talk with you about options. I'm going to be given the trip tickets for that day. I want to grab it after the final stop."

Mose nodded as he thought for a moment.

"All right," Mose began. "There are three components to an armored truck heist. First is the takeover, second is the response of law enforcement, and third is the getaway. Where's the final stop of the day?"

"Gemstone National Bank."

"Is it in a shopping center or is it a stand-alone?"

"Shopping Center," George told him. "But the driver's going to open his door. When he does, I figure we can take him out with a sniper's bullet from across the parking lot."

"That'll work, but you and your people have to move with military precision."

"What if I wanted to stop the truck, what do you suggest?"

"With either scenario," Mose explained, "you have to cut off communications. I've got a camouflage setup that will cut off the radio frequencies, GPS, and cellular phones. All you have to do is mount it on the roof of the armored truck."

"How do you get it up there?" George inquired.

"A drone," Mose answered. "Puts it up there and magnets hold it on."

"Where would a drone launch from?" George quizzed.

"I've got a van that's modified for you to take. You and your men can stand in the back of it. It's got a hatch on top to let the drone out."

As Mose spoke, George nodded his head affirmatively.

"What about stopping the truck?"

"You can't blow out the tires or put down spike strips. The rims have a rubber inlay to allow the truck to keep moving. You can hit the tires with a rocket-propelled grenade. That'll stop the truck, but it will also break the axle. So, you'll have to offload it wherever it stops."

"No other way?" George quizzed.

"Let me tell you about this other thing that I got."

Mose walked over one aisle and removed what looked like a steel block. It was twelve by twelve inches and two inches thick. It also had four small, circular metal legs.

"I call this device 'Confetti,' because that's all that is usually left after it goes off. It was originally designed as a car bomb. It's a cocktail of various plastic explosives and dynamite. Drives the bomb squad's nuts because that think a bomber is loyal to a particular type of explosive. My original thought with this thing is that if you could place it on the hood of the armored truck and set it off, maybe you would be able to either damage the truck or convince the crew that it would be in their best interest to stop."

George took the device from Mose to feel the weight of it.

"Would you just throw it on the hood?" George wondered.

"No. Use the drone. But, here's the problem. A couple of guys tried it for a heist of an armored truck down in Wyoming. It was so powerful that when it blew down into the engine, it broke the engine off its mounts. The truck stopped. No time to offload it."

"What about a smaller version of it?" George again posed an inquiry.

"If you want to try it, I'll do it," Mose assured him.

"Yeah, I want to try it," George told him.

"Another thing. If it's slow on the Interstate, the State Police will give the armored trucks an escort. Just be aware of that."

"Okay," George acknowledged.

"A couple of other things that I got for you," Mose shared as he walked down the aisle several yards.

He picked up a steel circle with a four-inch diameter that was recessed on one side and handed it to George.

"These are covers for the gun ports on the side of the truck," Mose advised. "See the liquid stuff around the perimeter, that's like Crazy Glue. The magnet only needs to hold it in place and in two seconds, they'll be locked on."

"That's gotta be done by hand, right?" George wondered.

"Yeah," Mose concurred. "The final thing I got for you is grenades. I got smokers and I got frags. The grenades I have are a lot more powerful that anything you have dealt with before. The frags will blow a room apart with the accompanying fireball. They will kill anybody who is in the room. What's unique about them is that they have an electronic activator. You can set it to blow five seconds after it leaves your hand or you can set it to detonate with a handheld detonator."

"I'll take a dozen of those," George advised and thought for a moment. "You got anything to go through bulletproof glass?"

"What year is the truck?" Mose asked.

"Either 2007 or 2004."

"The best thing for that is a powerful weapon, like a Taurus Raging Bull, .454 caliber Casull revolver. I suggest you keep hammering on the same area of the glass until the driver decides that it's in his best interest to stop the truck. I've got that gun here and I can give you a couple of speedloaders."

"Can you believe all the bullshit you gotta go through?" George opined.

"I will never understand why these guards want to get killed for three dollars an hour over minimum wage," Mose wondered.

"Crazy, huh?" George concluded.

"I may have a punch key for you, if the truck is a GMC," Mose realized. "Hey, can you still get those seats for the Broncos?"

"Yeah. Just tell me what games you want to go to," George told him.

"I want to find out when they're playing New England," Mose replied anxiously. "Did you see that new backup quarterback that Denver got? That guy's arm is like a rocket. Hey, come on. Let me show you the weapons that I have."

George continued his shopping and with Mose's guidance, moral support, and confidence, he was now prepared to take down the Mondo Run.

CHAPTER 30

As Roger Legion traversed the sidewalks of downtown San Diego on his way back to the America's Finest City Building, his mind was in full battle mode. Roger knew that his greatest source of power came from information. Information that could be used both as a shield and a sword.

Legion retrieved his cell phone and located the number for Glenn Edgarian, his 'go-to' private investigator, who was a master in the art of information collection. Glenn's track record with Roger was stellar and he never disappointed him.

"Glenn," Roger said immediately as he heard Glenn's voice. "This is Roger Legion."

"Roger, how are you?" Glenn asked with enthusiasm.

"You keeping busy?" Roger inquired.

"I'm never too busy for you," Glenn assured him.

"That's good to hear. I want you to do a background investigation on someone. Real thorough." Roger's voice took on an ominous tone.

"What's the name?"

"Daisy Zacaro. I think it's Z-A-C-A-R-O."

"I know the name. She works in the Federal AGs office." Glenn was referring to the US Attorney General's office. "They call her Crazy Daisy."

"I think that name fits her to a tee," Roger assessed. "Can you put this on the front burner?"

"Absolutely. I'll begin as soon as we hang up. Any special instructions or cost restrictions?" Glenn wondered.

"Do the necessary," Roger advised.

Glenn knew from Roger's urgency that cost was not a concern in this instance.

"It shall be done," Glenn told him. With that, the call was ended.

At that point, Roger was crossing in front of the old courthouse on Broadway when he saw a homeless man dragging a small dog by its leash. The dog was a twelve-pound beagle that was white and brown with a black accent on its back.

The homeless man wore pants and a sweatshirt that were so filthy and stained that it was impossible to determine their original color. The man's hair was so dirty, it looked like it was greased back with Crisco. He had a beard that protruded out like a giant Brillo pad. His foul odor wafted from one half block away.

When Roger saw that the dog was in distress, he pounced into action.

"HEY!" Legion yelled, getting the attention of nearly everyone on the block.

The homeless man looked at Legion, but continued to pull on the dog. Roger ran up to him to stop him.

"How much for the dog?" The way Legion said it, it sounded more like a demand than a question.

The homeless man looked up and down at Roger's suit and was about to walk away and again drag the dog. Roger grabbed the leash and snapped it out of the homeless man's hand.

"That's my dog!" the man yelled.

"I said, 'How much for the dog?'" Legion was firm in his reiteration.

The homeless man again looked at Legion in frustration.

"One thousand dollars," the man blurted out.

Roger stared him directly with his steel-blue eyes and as he did, he reached into one of his pants pockets and pulled out a money clip. He peeled off 2 one-hundred dollar bills and let them fall to the ground in front of the homeless man.

"That should be enough to get you coked out," Roger told him with an angry snarl.

"I'm gonna call the cops," the homeless man threatened.

"Why don't you do it?" Legion reassured him. "And we'll see who gets arrested."

The homeless man looked at Legion and then bent down to pick up the two hundred dollars.

"Come on, little girl," Roger said as he swooped down and picked up the dog, carrying her back to the office.

Roger called his wife to come and pick up the dog, but not before a generous helping of special treats and roast beef. The puppy would be taken to a luxury canine shelter in Northern San Diego County, called Kisses & Tummy Rubs.

If anyone wanted to move Roger Legion to violence, all they had to do was abuse a dog in front of him.

CHAPTER 31

Coeur d'Alene is the largest city and the county seat of Kootenai County, Idaho. Located thirty miles east of Spokane, Washington, Coeur d'Alene covers approximately sixteen square miles and has a population of approximately 46,400. It is the largest city in the Idaho panhandle.

George Lorin and his crew took an opportunity to engage in some celebratory activity with a four-hundred-dollar steak dinner before heading to the home of the men. At this point, none of the men knew any of the details and George refused to share any information until he knew he was in a private, safe location.

Garmin Simmons, referred to as "Gar," lived on North Fifth Street, near Hazel Avenue. This was a neighborhood of older, small, single-story homes, but they were not congested. Gar's home was approximately 1200 square feet, but he also had a detached, three stall garage that was approximately the same size as the house. The garage was the men's destination.

The inside of the garage was rather basic, but the walls were covered with Auralex wall insulation. This allowed the garage to be soundproof from the interior and exterior.

Gar gave everyone a folding chair and the four men, Smitty, Floyd, Rollo, and Gar, sat in a straight line next to each other. George took his position facing the four men.

"Armored truck," was all George said and allowed it to sink in. "You in or you out?"

"In," Smitty said immediately. As soon as he said it, the other three men followed suit.

"Good," George proclaimed. "The Friday before Labor Day, they got a big haul they refer to as the Mondo Run. I will have access to the trip tickets. After they make their last pickup, we're gonna take it over. It'll be up in Sandpoint. We'll have some very good technology and automatic weapons. We got to be smooth and we have to be precise. If you don't think you can do it, let me know. No hard feelings."

The men looked at each other, but none of them said a word.

"Smitty, I'm going to need you to take a shot about two hundred feet away. You'll have a rifle with a suppressor and subsonic ammunition."

The suppressor and subsonic ammunition would minimize the sound of the bullet being shot.

"How are you going to get him to open the door?"

"He's going to do it for us. The guy smokes like a chimney. The doors on an armored truck have a sensor, so whoever is monitoring it back at the home base knows when the door is open. This guy takes a magnetic strip, places it over the sensor and opens the door. He opens it just enough, so that the smoke and ashes go outside the truck. That's when you gotta take him."

Smitty nodded affirmatively.

"It shall be done."

"Gar, you and I are going to dress like an old man. We are going to wear the exact same outfit. We're going to wear a mask from a prop company in Hollywood. Once the driver's taken out, we're in the truck. Rollo, you will be dressed like a janitor that works at the shopping center. You keep an eye on the two boy scouts who go into the bank. Floyd, you are going to monitor the radio."

All the men were impressed with George's direct, concise presentation.

"You said we were going to have automatic weapons. What's the status on collateral damage?" Gar asked.

Gar was referring to the possible injury or death of innocent bystanders.

"We have to focus on the objective. If someone gets between us and the objective, then they have to be removed, right?"

"Damn straight," Smitty chimed in.

George's crew was now in place. They would rehearse their activity every day for the next four weeks. George would guide and micro-manage every aspect of the heist.

CHAPTER 32

Ruby's Diner is a nostalgia-driven hamburger and French fry restaurant with a 1940s motif. The booths are covered in bright, red vinyl and the walls are white with poster advertisements for Coca-Cola from sixty years earlier. The waitresses dress in red-and-white striped uniforms and most have their hair up in a bouffant style.

Ned Chandler was already seated and reviewing the menu when Brian Stensler entered. Ned wore a black t-shirt and jeans. Brian had a plaid, button shirt with an open collar and navy blue Dockers pants.

Brian joined Ned in a booth near the far end of the restaurant.

"Hey, what's going on?" Ned inquired.

"I got a killer parking space right near the escalator," Brian shared.

"Sweet," Ned responded. As he did a waitress appeared at the table.

"Can I get a drink order started for you?" she asked.

"I'll have a Coke," Ned told her.

"Do you have lemonade?" Brian wondered.

"Yes, we do," she responded.

"I'll take one of those."

"You guys ready to order?" she quizzed.

"I'll have a Ruby burger with cheese," Ned told her.

"Is cheddar cheese all right?"

"Yeah."

"It comes with French fries."

"That's fine," Ned assured her.

"How 'bout you?" she requested, turning her attention to Brian.

"I'll have the same."

The waitress smiled and walked away. Ned gave a quick glance around the restaurant before he began to speak. He repositioned himself in the booth to move his head closer to Brian.

"This is what's going to happen with the money," he began.

"First of all," Brian interrupted, "how much money is it now?"

"I don't know exactly, but it's at least seven hundred fifty thousand dollars. It could be a lot more by now."

"I'm a little uncomfortable that we have to fly blind with this thing. It's our deal and we are going to let our old friend, who we haven't seen in five years, control the cash?" Brian retorted with zeal.

"Look," Ned opined, "he's the guy who showed us how to finesse this thing. You know we couldn't pull it off without him. The work is done. You and I are going to get a nice little bump. We're just waiting on the payday." Ned looked at Brian as Brian rubbed the outside of his cheek. "What's wrong?"

"Oh, these goddamn braces. They're either cutting my tongue or cutting the inside of my cheek."

As he spoke, the same waitress appeared to deliver their drink order and moved on. Ned looked around quickly and began to disclose details.

"An order is going to go into the bank to have the entire balance of the account transferred offshore to a bank in Santa Lucia in the Caribbean. After that, it's going to Panama and Malta, until it finally ends up in Luxembourg. There's no way the Feds can trace it."

"Once it's offshore, we have no control," Brian responded with deadpan enthusiasm.

"We don't want control until we have our hands on it. Until then, there is no way they can trace us to it. You worry too much."

"What does worry me is your comment about the phones being tapped. Maybe the Feds are on to something now. And you can't underestimate Roger Legion. That guy is always ten steps ahead of everybody. I don't want to end up on that Memorial Plaque with the other dead lawyers. If he finds out about this, or our involvement, that's exactly where our names are going to end up. I know it," Brian spoke with a firm conviction.

"If he didn't find out after Roy Sims killed himself," Ned shared, "he's never going to find out. We did this right. According to the plan."

As Ned finished his sentenced, the waitress returned with the food.

Brian could not shake his uneasy feeling with the plan. He felt like an incriminating piece of evidence was left at the scene of the crime, even though he could not think of what that might be. He was sure that if anyone could find it, it would be Roger Legion.

CHAPTER 33

THE FRIDAY BEFORE LABOR DAY

Dash's right-hand man, Pierre, met George in the parking lot of the Monarch Mountain Coffee Shop at 7:00 am to provide him with the trip tickets. George reviewed them quickly and found that the last stop was as Dash had informed him, the Gemstone National Bank on East Superior Street. The pickup time was set for 2:38 pm.

"Good luck," Pierre told him with his thick, French accent and both men proceeded to their cars.

George returned to a motel where he and his men were staying called the Meandering Moose, on South Marion Avenue in Sandpoint. Earlier that morning, they all had breakfast at the local Jack in the Box restaurant.

George and Gar turned their attention to their disguises. George had obtained latex masks from a Hollywood prop company, under a false name, and had his buddy, Mose, his criminal sundries supplier, modified the masks so that the wiring for the closed-circuit walkie-talkie was inside the mask. George had studied application techniques for similar latex masks used in films and he assisted Gar using spirit gum, an adhesive used primarily for affixing costume prosthetics.

George also applied makeup around his eyes and Gar's eyes and they also wore human-looking gloves that made their hands appear more aged.

Now they looked identical: old and wrinkled, bald and craggy. They both wore light brown khaki Dockers pants, a black t-shirt under a green, checkered button shirt that was buttoned to the neck, a plain, green baseball cap and wire rimmed sunglasses.

Before putting on the final item, a green sport coat, they put on shoulder holsters that contained a Sig Sauer P320 semi-automatic pistol. The gun was a 9 mm caliber and contained seventeen rounds in the magazine. Each holster carried an additional two magazines.

"How did you come up with this idea?" Gar asked as George secured Gar's earpiece, within the mask, into his ear.

"Did you ever hear of the Geezer Bandit?" George inquired. "This is how he did it."

As George finished his sentence, the remaining three men walked in. Smitty stared at both of them in awe.

"Holy shit," Smitty uttered with a smile. "They are not gonna know what hit 'em."

"Smitty," George began his command. "You and Floyd take the van and set up residence in the parking lot next to the bank in the space that we talked about. Don't get out of the van. You want something, call us and we will bring it to you. Floyd, you start monitoring the police bands. You guys see or hear anything suspicious, get ahold of me."

"Roger, that," Smitty told him.

"Gar and Rollo are going to come with me. We are going to check up on some of the other pickups based on these trip tickets. We are also going to check the location that's set up for the transfer from the armored truck to our transfer truck. We'll get that truck in place."

Smitty and Floyd left and time was moving quickly. Rollo put on his janitor overalls and a pair of sunglasses. Within his overalls, Rollo had a belt holster that allowed him to carry the same Sig Sauer gun as George and Gar.

"Gar," George spoke up. "You are going to have to lie down in the back seat of the car. I don't want anyone to get antsy if they see two of us."

Gar nodded in agreement.

"Did you guys check out of your room?" George asked.

"Yeah," Rollo answered.

"Okay. I'm going to check out for this room," George spoke as he raised the telephone receiver and pressed one button on the phone.

It was 11:00 am. There was approximately three and one-half hours until the conclusion of the Mondo Run.

CHAPTER 34

Thursday morning arrived and the lobby of the America's Finest City Building was a plethora of activity. It consisted of highly polished brown marble with a twenty-foot-high vaulted ceiling, a concierge station, and the America's Finest City News, which allowed a visitor the opportunity to purchase a newspaper or refreshment.

One of the unique features of the elevators within the building was that anyone who boarded an elevator on the first floor of the lobby or the parking garage was able to take a nonstop ride directly to their destination. A passenger would request the destination on a kiosk and a voice would announce your elevator's arrival and proposed destination.

There were twenty-four elevator banks in the America's Finest City Building and three elevator banks would be dedicated to three floors within the building.

Two police detectives, a male and female, from the Homicide Division of the San Diego Police Department entered the building and walked directly to a kiosk to request a ride to the twenty-fourth floor.

When their elevator was announced, they entered and were the lone passengers. The man was Detective Peter Atherton. He was thirty-two years old, five feet ten inches tall, with an athletic build. He had black, curly hair, clean-shaven, and wore a black sport coat from Joseph A. Banks, with black Dockers pants, blue shirt, and dark, blue tie. He was married with three children, all girls, one of which was autistic.

The woman was Detective Margaret Byrne. She was in her early forties, slender, but not petite. She sported blonde, shoulder-length hair and dressed in a blue, Ralph Lauren single-button blazer with matching slacks and a white shirt with blue piping. She had a reputation for being good with a gun. Her face displayed a calmness, which, to the uninitiated, may indicate inner peace. But her visage was a façade. She was quiet, all business. The kind of woman you just knew was brimming with secrets.

Margaret had been on the police force for eight years, the last five in the Homicide Division. Pete had been a detective for one month and Margaret was his first partner.

"This is a nice elevator," Pete observed.

The elevator floor and walls contained the same marble as found in the lobby. The doors were gold-colored stainless steel. Around the perimeter of the three solid walls, a stainless steel circular bar protruded approximately four inches from the wall for a passenger to hold during their ride.

On the door side of the elevator, approximately five feet off the ground was a small television monitor, which informed the passenger of news headlines, the time of day and the weather. Under the monitor was a control keyboard for simple door functions, an emergency stop, and a telephone pad to call for help or other functions of the elevator.

"I haven't been in this building for the past five years," Margaret acknowledged.

"This is where the famous shootout took place?" Peter wondered with enthusiasm.

"My partner, Fred Saydah, said we'd only be up in Legion's office for a couple of minutes," Margaret recalled, looking forward and deep in thought. "When the elevator doors opened, it sounded like a shooting range. Fred barreled into that room blind. We had no idea what was going on. He tells me to call for backup and I tell him to wait. But Fred always did what he wanted to do."

"Did you go in after him?" Pete inquired, hanging on to Margaret's every word.

"No. Before I could even dial 9-1-1, he flew back through a glass door after taking a load of buckshot to the gut. I took Fred's gun and this lawyer and I opened up on the last guy. I was firing so fast, you would have thought I had a machine gun. When it was over, ten people were dead and Roger Legion, who was in the room, didn't even have a scratch on him. And he never touched a gun."

"How long did Fred last?" Pete asked.

"He was dead two hours later" Margaret shared. "He got what he was looking for, an exit."

As she finished her sentence, they arrived on the twenty-fourth floor. They exited the elevator and walked directly to Nina, the receptionist. When they caught Nina's eye, she stopped to speak with them.

"May I help you?" Nina asked.

Pete could not help but look around the palatial lobby in awe.

"We'd like to speak with Roger Legion," Margaret told her. "I'm Detective Margaret Byrne. This is Detective Peter Atherton. San Diego Police Department."

"Do you have an appointment?"

"No, we don't," Margaret responded.

"One moment, please."

Nina pressed two buttons and Roger Legion answered.

"Yes."

"Detectives Margaret Byrne and Peter Atherton are here to see you. They don't have an appointment."

Legion wondered why police detectives were coming to visit. Perhaps it dealt with the firm's information technology person's suicide.

"Show them into the conference room. I'll be right there."

CHAPTER 35

Inside Henri's Haberdashery, on the second floor, Dash looked aimlessly at a computer screen in his office and forgot why he was looking at the screen. Dash wore a black suit made of Vanquish II fabric, a cloth produced in the United Kingdom that uses blends of some of the rarest fibers in the world, including qiviuk, pashmina, and vicuna. The stitching was made of white gold.

He also wore a light blue shirt with a dark, blue tie and matching pocket square handkerchief.

Tex appeared at the doorway to Dash's office, wearing the same cowboy outfit that he wore when Dash first met George.

"Monitor the police radio," Dash told him. "I want to know when it happens. Did they set up the perimeter?"

"They're going to do it," Tex advised. "But they think they should focus on the other truck. The one actually making the Mondo Run."

"No," Dash warned. "There should be no extra police presence for that truck. There is a plan in place to empty it before it gets back to the base."

"Do you think your friend is really gonna shoot it out?" Tex wondered.

"Our friend, George, is sure of himself. That's what makes him susceptible and fallible. In his mind, he's not going to prison, so he's foolish enough to believe he can take on the State Police. Even if he is still alive in a few hours, this will be his last day on earth."

The way Dash spoke, he was the one who sounded sure of himself. The clock was ticking and soon, the Mondo Run, would be complete.

CHAPTER 36

As Roger Legion proceeded to the conference room, he realized that one of the detective's names sounded familiar. Roger met Detective Margaret Byrne five years earlier, when she and her partner, Fred Saydah, were investigating the murder of an insurance claims manager. He also recalled that she was in the conference room and assisted in ending the madness that day when a firefight erupted.

Legion entered the conference room and saw the two detectives admiring the view from the twenty-fourth floor.

"Hello, I'm Roger Legion."

"Mr. Legion, I'm Detective Byrne and this is Detective Atherton. We're from the Homicide Division, San Diego Police Department."

"How have you been Detective Byrne? It's been a long time."

The comment brought a smile to Margaret's face.

"So, you do remember?" she said.

"That day would be very hard to forget," Roger replied. "How can I help you?"

"Sir, did you know an attorney named Rike Hessler?" Peter asked.

Rike Hessler was the attorney representing an extortionist, who claimed to have photos of a CEO involved with child pornography. Kez Thomkins retained Roger's services to assist his company, Zunkunft, to pay off the extortionist.

"I know of Mr. Hessler, but I've never met him," Roger shared.

"He was found murdered last night in his apartment," Margaret shared staring at Legion for his reaction. "Two bullets to the head."

"That's unfortunate," Roger told her, maintaining a stoic poker face.

"The reason we're here, Mr. Legion," Detective Atherton shared, "is that your name was listed in his day planner. It indicated that you were going to have a four o'clock meeting with him today. Is that correct?"

"That is correct," Roger conveyed.

"Can you tell us about the nature of the meeting that you were going to have with him?" Margaret wondered.

"I'm afraid I can't. That information is privileged," Legion declared.

Margaret stared at Legion for a moment and then caught Peter's eye.

"Can I ask, when was the last time you spoke with Mr. Hessler?" Margaret quizzed.

"The day before yesterday. Around two o'clock in the afternoon."

"Do you know of anyone who might want him dead?" Margaret again inquired.

"Like I said, I never met the guy before. He was going to be coming here to the office to discuss one case that we have in common."

"Can you tell us at least the general nature of the case?" Peter re-asked Margaret's earlier question.

"I'm sorry, I can't."

Margaret once again stared at Legion and reached into her coat pocket. She pulled out a business card.

"If you think of anything that you can share with us, will you please call?" she requested as she handed him her business card.

"I will," Roger told her.

"Let's go," she declared to Peter. Legion watched them both exit the conference room.

The murder of Rike Hessler perplexed Roger. To resolve the situation involving Zunkunft, would he now have to deal with a murderer instead of an extortionist?

CHAPTER 37

George, Gar, and Rollo checked the small wooded area near Cocolalla Lake, in Idaho, just off US Highway 95. They drove a white, 2005 Chevy Impala. The plan was to transfer the money from the armored truck to their rented box truck at this location. It was quiet and the area could not be seen from the Interstate.

The men then proceeded to pick up the twelve-foot U-Haul box truck and drove it to an empty lot behind the Westmond Convenience Store & Deli, located in Westmond, Idaho. This was the closest commercial location to the transfer point.

They then proceeded to a Walmart Supercenter just north of Sandpoint in Ponderay, Idaho. This was the next pickup scheduled according to the trip tickets provided by Pierre to George. The store was crowded and parking was difficult.

George continued to drive around the parking lot until the Parapet Logistics Armored truck appeared. It was exactly on time, at 1:22 pm, and two of the armed guards exited the truck. One of the guards carried two large, leather money bags and the other carried a large coin bag that had wheels.

The fact that they were carrying bags into the store caused George concern.

"Do you see this Rollo?" George asked.

"What's going on?" Gar wondered from his position on the floor of the back seat.

"They're bringing stuff in," George shared. "They should be taking it out."

Both of the guards emerged from the store empty handed. George's face, under the latex mask, was flush. He was not having a good feeling about the Mondo Run.

"Let's go to the next stop."

The men then proceeded to the Horizon Credit Union on North Fifth Avenue in Sandpoint. The armored truck arrived and once again two guards emerged from the truck wheeling two coin cases into the bank. Within ten minutes, both guards returned empty handed.

George was getting pissed and he sensed betrayal.

"Where we going?" Rollo asked.

"Gemstone Bank," George replied.

The Gemstone National Bank was the planned location for the heist.

When they arrived at the bank, there was a flurry of activity from shoppers preparing for the long weekend. Rollo began sweeping errant trash from in front of the bank using a small broom and a dustpan with an extended handle, so he would not have to bend over. He would have looked very familiar to the regular customers because George took him to the bank nearly every day over the past several weeks to hone his craft.

Gar, dressed as an old geezer, began to simply walk around aimlessly, never letting the front doors of the bank out of his sight.

George found a parking space not far from the van where Smitty and Floyd were holed up. The van was a late model, gray, Mercedes-Benz Sprinter cargo van. It had an extended roofline that allowed 78.2 inches of standing room inside. The walls were covered with wall insulation to cancel any interior sounds to the exterior. There was also a gun cage, an ammunition cage, a power source for any electronics and a platform, behind the front seats of the vehicle, approximately three by three feet that could be raised or lowered. This would be the takeoff and landing point for the drone.

In the roof of the vehicle, above the moveable platform, was a powered sunroof to allow the drone to exit the vehicle. Inside the back doors of the van was a moveable carpeted shelf. This allowed a rifle to rest upon it for firing out of the vehicle. Small portions of the doors could be removed when the shot had to be taken.

George entered the van through the passenger door and stepped into the rear area where Smitty stood and waited. From the ceiling of the van were several handgrip metal circles that toggled back and forth like those on a subway train.

Smitty held an Accuracy International AX Covert sniper rifle. This gun was desert tan in color with a sixteen-inch barrel and chambered in 7.62 NATO rounds. It had a powerful scope and bipod legs on the barrel end of the gun.

Floyd sat on the floor with an Apple laptop computer listening to alternating police scans and for any comments regarding armored trucks.

"Something's not right," George told the men.

"What?" Smitty asked in a petulant tone.

George picked up a pair of binoculars and scanned the parking lot. The van looked like it had no windows, but it was also shrink wrapped in gray. It had a film on the windows that allowed the passengers to look out, but outsiders could not look in.

Then George saw what he feared. He saw a box truck parked several stores down from the bank. A security guard was having a discussion with the driver and it appeared that the driver was being asked to move the truck. George saw the driver show the security officer a badge.

"Rollo, Gar," George called out to them in a rushed tone through the walkie-talkie within his mask. "If you can hear me, wave your hand." Both men complied. "You guys get back to the car. Go to our rental truck. Don't move it until I tell you. This op has been compromised."

As soon as he finished speaking, Floyd spoke up.

"I know where they are," Floyd said with surety, looking up at George.

"Who?" George quizzed.

"The other armored truck. We were given their GPS frequency. I've been following them."

"Where are they?" George demanded with urgency.

Floyd typed several keys and a map appeared on the screen.

"They just got onto Highway 95 south. They have maybe a four-mile head start on us."

George looked at Smitty.

"What do you say?"

"Let's go," Smitty replied with deadpan certainty.

The van took off in high pursuit of what would ultimately be either their destiny or their demise.

CHAPTER 38

Just after 1:30 pm, Judge Harrison Ogilvie sat in his chambers in Department 61 of the San Diego Superior Court and scanned the day's edition of the Wall Street Journal. He was waiting to commence the afternoon docket. The Judge enjoyed making people wait, so that when he did arrive, his presence would be in greater demand.

The Judge's cell phone, which sat on his desk, began to ring. He picked it up to examine the Caller ID. It was a San Diego call, but he did not recognize the number. He felt a compulsion to answer it.

"Yes," he answered in a brusque tone.

"Harry. It's Daisy Zacaro."

"Oh, hello, Daisy. I didn't recognize the number."

"You should put it in your contacts list, because I plan on calling you on a regular basis. Now, what do you got for me?" Daisy wondered in anticipation.

"I need a little more time," the Judge pleaded.

"How did I know you were going to say that?" Daisy responded curtly.

"Listen, I'm still going to get you what you want. I'll get Legion on tape."

"One week. That's it. After that I'll call San Diego PD and I'll make sure there's a news crew around to film your perp walk. Understand?"

"Yes," he slowly replied.

"One thing I don't have is the luxury of time. I know Roger Legion is working on a strategy to stay out of jail. I can't let that happen."

"Speaking of strategy," the Judge interjected, "there's a private investigator asking questions about you."

"What's his name?"

"The guy's name is Glenn Edgarian. Works for Legion."

"Who cares?"

"Maybe you should. Edgarian's good. If he finds out about your connection to Legion, I believe your whole case will go right down the shitter."

There was a pause at Daisy's end.

"Don't worry about the investigator, Harry. I'll take care of him. Just worry about keeping your tight ass out of jail. And I shouldn't have to call you, you call me. If you don't come through on your part of the bargain, I will make sure every darkie in that jail gets a piece of you."

With that, Daisy disconnected the call.

Judge Ogilvie returned his cell phone to the desk top. He opened one of the desk drawers and pulled out an older Lanier handheld voice recorder. The device utilized micro-cassettes. He looked at it for a moment and set it down on the desk.

He then picked up the telephone handset and pushed one button. It was answered immediately.

"Edna, get me a list of all the cases we have in this department involving the Legion law firm. I need it immediately."

Judge Ogilvie felt like he was now in the jaws of a vice and Daisy was enjoying the tightening process. It was time for the Judge to evaluate all of his options.

CHAPTER 39

US Highway 95 is an undivided two-lane highway for most of its length in Idaho, covering five hundred thirty-eight miles. The Highway runs from the Mexican to the Canadian border through five western states. Through Idaho, it is mostly lined with forest trees allowing a vehicle to quickly disappear if so desired.

Smitty drove the gray van, provided by Mose, the supplier of weapons and technology for the job, at a breakneck speed. Floyd, sitting on the floor of the van, was monitoring the GPS location of the armored truck that the men believed actually had the contents of the Mondo Run. George stood in the van, holding a metal ring, which hung from the ceiling that would assist a person to stand. He stared out the front of the van for their prize.

"We're less than a mile away," Floyd told them.

"Get the drone ready," George told Floyd.

Floyd proceeded to the raised platform in the center of the truck, turned the drone on, and unlocked it from four metal clips that secured it to the platform.

"Smitty," George spoke in a raised voice, "Once Floyd cuts off the communications, I need you to pull up along the side of the truck and keep pace with it."

"Got it!" Smitty acknowledged. This would require Smitty to drive against any traffic on this two-lane highway.

As they rounded a bend in the road, they saw the object of their desire. It was a 2004 GMC C6500 Griffin Armored Truck. It was gray in color and the words 'Parapet Logistics' were written on all four sides of the vehicle. Less than one-quarter mile ahead of the armored truck, was an Idaho State police car with two officers providing an escort for the Mondo Run.

"Open the hatch! Get the drone up!" George barked orders like a military commander.

As soon as the hatch opened, Floyd sent the drone out carrying the device that would camouflage GPS, cellular and radio transmissions. Almost immediately, George could see that the drone was about to drop its cargo on the top of the armored truck.

"Floyd, as soon as you can, cut 'em," George yelled referring to the truck's communications. "Smitty, pull up beside it."

Smitty moved the truck into position at 63 mph and George slid open the side door of the van, nearest the armored truck. George hung out the door and slapped the first gun port cover on the armored truck. This was a recessed metal circular device that was magnetic and created by Mose's research and development people. Around the surface area where the device stuck to the truck, it was covered with a 'Super Glue'-type substance.

George then pulled himself back into the van and grabbed a second gun port cap.

"Smitty, pull it up about five feet!" George screamed.

As Smitty pulled forward, hoping that no traffic was heading toward him, the crew of the armored truck were now aware that they were under siege. Two members tried frantically to raise someone on either the radio or their cellular phone. The third crew member grabbed a Colt M4 carbine rifle and tried to open the gun port that

George had covered. He was unable to get the cover off. He considered shooting it, but did not know what the bullet would do in such a confined area. He didn't try the other gun port because he assumed it would also be covered.

"HIT THE HORN!" yelled the crew member handling the M4. "Get the cops attention!" The driver pushed on the horn for a loud, steady blare.

As soon as the horn commenced, George stood up on the platform within the truck, with his head and shoulders out of the hatch, looking at the State Police car.

"Floyd, give me the RPG!"

Floyd handed George a rocket-propelled grenade launcher. George immediately leveled the weapon and sighted it, aiming it in the center of the rear of the police cruiser, just above the bumper. The ordinance sailed through the air and struck its target with deadly precision.

When the grenade exploded, it created a hellacious fireball, which consumed the car. The explosion lifted the car off its rear tires to a point where it stood perpendicular to the ground for a moment and pirouetted off the highway onto the side of the road where it burned unabated.

The crew of the armored truck focused on the explosion while George fastened the second gun port cover on the truck.

"George," Floyd called out. "We got traffic coming up behind us.

George looked to the north and could see the traffic in the far distance. He moved to the passenger seat of the van and opened the glove box. Within the glove box was a control panel to operate several additional secrets of this van.

"Smitty, I want you to let him get ahead of us, then drive right down the center of the road. Floyd," George called out for his attention, "get the drone back in here."

Both men complied. George was able to watch the road behind them on the backup camera that would normally go on only when the vehicle was in reverse. When Smitty had the van centered in the middle of the road, George pushed a button that was marked, 'S.S.' From the back of the van, a set of spike strips deployed onto the highway. They pushed down off the van with pneumatic force, so they dug into the pavement and locked in place. Once secured, a wing of spike strips popped open on each side to allow the spike strips to cover the entire two lanes of the highway.

George moved like a man on fire with whatever emotions he was displaying covered by his Old Geezer mask. From the gun cabinet, he retrieved the Taurus Raging Bull, .454 caliber Casull revolver and two loaded speed loaders. The drone was now back in the van.

"Get the Confetti on the drone," George ordered and Floyd began to set it up.

The Confetti was an explosive device, originally designed as a car bomb, which was built to supposedly disable the truck without causing extensive damage. It would allow the truck to be moved. This version of the Confetti was a smaller model and this was the first time it was actually being used in a criminal heist.

George again returned to the passenger seat.

"Smitty, remember what we talked about with this .454 Casull revolver? The kick is stronger than a .44 magnum, but it kicks back toward you, not up in the air. You got it?"

"Yeah," Smitty acknowledged.

"You want me to drive?" George asked.

"No. I'm more stationery here. Watch the road and take over the wheel."

"Aim at the driver through the side window," George told him. "Wherever it hits, use that as your target for the next shot. That's how we'll get through the glass."

Now the drone was up in the air, hovering over the hood of the truck. George wanted the Confetti as close to the windshield as possible. Floyd dropped the Confetti and it landed within three inches of the windshield, right in the center of the truck's hood.

Smitty rolled down his window and the truck's crew members could see his monstrous revolver. George locked eyes with the driver and mouthed the words, 'Stop the truck.' The crew discussed it, but did not stop the truck.

"Floyd, light'em up."

With three keystrokes, Floyd detonated the Confetti. A massive fireball erupted on the hood of the truck and it caused the hood to bend into the engine compartment. In addition, when the explosion occurred, it acted as a braking system for the truck. It pushed the truck into the ground, while the momentum of the truck lifted the rear end nearly a foot off the ground and dropped it. The explosion placed a vertical crack in the one and one-quarter inch, latex glass windshield.

Smitty pulled the van up parallel to the armored truck and extended his arm out the window toward the passenger window of the armored truck, aiming at the driver's head. George suddenly screamed.

"LOOK OUT!"

From around a curve came a late model Jeep Wrangler at high speed. Neither the armored truck nor the van took any evasive action. The Jeep cut in front of both of them in an attempt to avoid a collision. The front driver-side bumper of the armored truck caught the side of the Jeep under the Jeep's passenger-side running board, which lifted and tipped the Jeep over.

Smitty commenced his barrage on the glass. With each hit, the armored truck was rocked by the power of the bullet. After the fifth bullet hit, there was a hole in the glass and the truck began to slow down.

The armored truck stopped just south of Athol, Idaho. The van parked immediately in front of it, on the side of the road. Smitty got out of the van and pointed his gun at the driver. George emerged from the van carrying a larger Confetti device and placed it right against the windshield of the truck.

The side door of the truck opened and all three men exited with their hands in the air. Smitty took over driving duties of the armored truck and took off. The truck was stopped for less than five minutes.

The three armored truck crew members entered the van and were duct taped, while their hands were secured with zip ties. Both vehicles drove down the road approximately one-half mile, before Smitty spotted an old mining road. He pulled in and George called Gar and Rollo to arrange for their rendezvous.

Gar and Rollo were there with the transfer truck within twenty minutes. The men were able to offload the contents of the Mondo Run into the U-Haul truck in less than fifteen minutes.

Gar and Rollo took off to a storage locker in Coeur d'Alene where they planned to store their booty until they divided it up.

At the transfer point, George had the three crew members loaded back into the armored truck. He turned to Smitty and ordered, "Start the van."

Smitty watched George's action from his side rear-view mirror and Floyd looked through the back windows of the van. George had removed a three-gallon container from the van. He climbed onto the top of the armored truck and emptied the contents of the container. It was filled with kerosene.

George then took one of Mose's special grenades that could be detonated immediately or remotely in hand. He opened the side door of the armored truck and tossed it in. He then walked back to the passenger side door of the van and got in.

"Let's go," he told Smitty nonchalantly.

As they pulled out of the forested area and when George could see the road in sight, he detonated the grenade. The truck became a raging inferno that would continue to burn until the FBI arrived.

CHAPTER 40

As the afternoon began to wane at Legion & Associates, Roger Legion spent the majority of the day reviewing the files that were selected by Unibility Insurance for a legal audit that was set to take place within the next ten days. Roger's friend, Doc, told Roger that the audit would be conducted by undercover FBI agents looking into mail and wire fraud.

It was 3:55 pm on this Thursday afternoon, when a call came in from the receptionist.

"Yes," Roger answered.

"Rike Hessler is here to see you," answered Nina.

Roger was frozen. Earlier that day, he was visited by two detectives from the Homicide Division of the San Diego Police Department advising him that Rike Hessler had been murdered. Roger was scheduled to meet with him today day at 4:00 pm.

"Show him into the conference room," Roger requested.

Legion rolled back in his chair and removed a business card from his inside coat pocket. He dialed the handwritten number on the back of the card. It was answered on the second ring.

"Margaret Byrne," the voice revealed.

"Detective Byrne, this is Roger Legion. A man just showed up in the lobby of my office claiming to be Rike Hessler."

"Mr. Legion, keep him there. We're on our way," Margaret's voice pulsed urgency.

Roger then proceeded down the hallway from his office and entered the conference room.

"Good afternoon, Mr. Hessler. I'm Roger Legion."

Roger walked up to the man and met him with a smile and a firm handshake.

"It's a pleasure to meet you," the man said with a slight hint of a German accent.

He was in his late 30s, thin, five feet eleven inches tall and wore a cheap, dark wool suit. His brown hair was close-cropped on the sides and puffed up on top, being combed to the side. His black tie was off-center on his neck and he had two days of beard growth.

"I'm glad you could make it," Roger shared with him. "Let's sit down."

Roger sat on the side of the table with his back facing the windows. The other man sat at the end of the table closest to the door where he entered.

"Well, Mr. Legion, I wish to conclude our business in as expeditious of a manner as possible. Shall we proceed?" the man inquired, with his voice succinct and sounding out each syllable of his sentence.

"My client is willing to pay you for the items you have for sale," Roger conveyed, "but we have a few conditions. First, I would like to see one of the photos, so that I can have it examined to determine if it is genuine."

"I would expect nothing less," the man replied and placed his briefcase in front of him. He opened it and retrieved an envelope, which he handed to Legion.

147

"Second, we are going to need your client to sign a contract, including a confidentiality agreement, agreeing that there are no other copies of the photos in existence and ..."

Before Legion could finish his sentence, the doors of the conference room burst open and Detectives Byrne and Atherton bolted into the room with their guns drawn aimed at the man claiming to be Rike Hessler.

"FREEZE!" Both detectives yelled the word in sync.

Pete came in through the door closest to the man, who made a slight twitch toward him as if considering a quick exit out of the room. Pete's semi-automatic, .45 caliber, Smith & Wesson M & P 45 handgun changed his mind immediately.

"Keep your hands where I can see them," Pete told him. "Stand up. Hands up against the wall. Feet back and spread 'em."

Margaret motioned to Legion to step over to her end of the room. He complied and she kept her Sig Sauer, semi-automatic, .9 millimeter pistol trained on the man while Pete patted him and placed him in handcuffs. Pete read him his rights while Margaret spoke to Legion.

"Are you all right?" she asked.

"I'm fine," Legion responded with a smile as if it was no big deal.

"Are we going to transport him?" Pete asked.

"No," Margaret replied. "Take him downstairs. We'll call a black and white with a cage. You go ahead. I want to talk to Mr. Legion."

Margaret was indicating that she wanted Pete to call for a black and white patrol car with a contained back seat for prisoner transport.

"Mr. Legion," the man spoke up as he was being escorted out of the room. "I apologize for this misunderstanding. I will contact you so that we can conclude our business."

"All right," Legion answered.

Pete took the man into the lobby and they both boarded an elevator.

"Thanks for calling us," Margaret conveyed with gratitude. "I didn't want to say anything in front of him that you called."

"I appreciate that," Roger shared with her.

"Are you sure you can't tell me anything about why he was here?"

"I'm afraid I can't," Legion responded. "But if he decides to talk, would you please call me immediately?"

"Absolutely," she assured him.

He walked her to the reception area and to the center elevator. Legion pushed a button to call a ride for her. Margaret decided to speak up.

"Can I call you Roger?"

"Sure. May I call you Margaret?'

Margaret put her hand out to shake his hand.

"It's a deal," she confirmed.

Just then a bell rang announcing the arrival of the center elevator. Roger Legion stood within two feet of the golden elevator doors as they began to open, and then everything seemed to move in slow motion.

Roger turned from talking to Margaret and he could see red blood splatter on the back wall of the elevator and Margaret immediately went into meltdown mode.

"PETE! NO! NO! NOOOOOOO!"

Roger had placed his foot against the door of the elevator to keep it from closing while he struggled with Margaret to keep her back from entering the elevator.

"No, Margaret, you can't go in there. NINA!" Roger yelled to the receptionist. "Call 9-1-1! We need an ambulance and the police over here right away!"

Margaret began to sob incessantly and nearly dropped to her knees while being held by Roger. He reached into the elevator and hit the emergency stop button, which would keep the elevator door open and keep the elevator in place.

Inside the elevator, Detective Pete Atherton was nearly on the floor, but he was handcuffed behind his back with the handcuffs around the handrail at the rear of the elevator car. This held his body slightly off the floor. He was shot twice in the back of the head with his own gun, which was on the floor of the elevator. His hollow point bullets took his forehead and the top of his skull completely off. His head looked like a chalice that was off center and blood was dripping over the edge and down the front of his face.

"Roger," Margaret pulled on his suitcoat to get his attention. "Call downstairs," she spoke quickly while attempting to resume her composure. "Tell them to lockdown the building. Give them a description of the guy. Call 9-1-1 back and tell them an officer is down and we need to set up a perimeter around the building."

Roger helped her to a seat on one of the couches in the lobby and then began to comply with her requests. The case that his client wanted to keep quiet, just broke the sound barrier.

CHAPTER 41

George, Smitty, and Floyd met up with Gar and Rollo at a pre-arranged storage locker in Coeur d'Alene. The locker was large enough for a small car to drive into it. They offloaded the contents of the rental truck into the locker and locked it with a lock provided by the storage facility. George also placed a motion sensor on the door, so that he would be alerted if anyone touched the door.

All five men stood in front of the door with smiles, even though you could not see a smile on George's face or Gar's face due to the latex masks they wore.

"Rollo, Floyd," George directed. "You guys bring the rental truck back. Then you're done for the day. Let's get together tomorrow. Here. Eleven o'clock. We'll figure out what the take down was."

Both men nodded their heads. Floyd drove the rental truck and Rollo walked to the front of the lot to drive the white, 2005 Chevy Impala.

"Gar, Smitty, you guys come with me," George told them.

"Where we going?" Gar wondered.

"I gotta go see a guy about a suit," George answered. "Let's go."

Smitty and Gar followed George to the front parking area of the storage facility where they had parked the van they just used to take down the Mondo Run.

"Can I take the mask off?" Gar asked.

"Keep it on until we finish this last thing," George told him.

They entered the van, with Smitty driving, and traveled back to Sandpoint. Along the way, they passed through the traffic congestion caused by their earlier activity. The men saw the area where firetrucks were parked on the highway, but the armored truck could not be seen from the street. Further up the highway, they saw the spot where the burned out police cruiser had met its final resting place. The men simply looked, without a word, like all the other rubbernecking travelers.

When they reached Sandpoint, they cruised down North Division Street to the thirteen hundred block and the home of Henri's Haberdashery. The parking lot was empty with the exception of Dash's white Mercedes-Benz S550.

The van passed the building and George got out of his seat and walked to the gun cage within the van. He retrieved a Heckler & Koch MP7 submachine gun and two additional clips for the gun. Each clip, including the clip in the gun, held forty bullets. This gun fired 4.6×30 mm ammunition at a rate of 950 rounds per minute. The ammunition of this gun is unique because it is made almost entirely out of hardened steel to defeat body armor. George also picked up a leather bag that contained eleven of the twelve grenades he obtained from his friend, Mose.

Smitty pulled in near the street end of the Henri's Haberdashery parking lot and stopped the van.

"Drop Gar off in the back. There's a heavy metal door back there. That's the only other way out of the building. Anybody comes out other than me, kill'em." Smitty nodded in compliance. "You see any cops, grab Gar and get out of here. I'll be all right."

George stepped out of the van and walked in a straight line to the front door. When he was within twenty feet of the door, he raised the machine gun and pulled the trigger. He strafed the glass of the front door and the bullets decimated it, allowing him to walk right in.

He proceeded to the glass display of the suit that Dash had created for the former Prime Minister of Canada and unleashed the power of the machine gun upon it. It tore the fine fabrics to shreds as the suit was ripped into unrecognizable pieces.

There were four rooms on each floor and the first floor also contained a walk-in refrigerator for furs. George tossed a grenade into the first room on the left and then he moved to the first room on the right and tossed a second grenade into it. Within seconds of throwing the grenades, they detonated, shaking the building and utilizing everything in the room as a fuel source. The explosions also destroyed the sprinkler heads, not allowing them to work properly.

Dash was in his second floor office with Tex, his muscle man. He had been watching George's activity on closed-circuit monitors.

"Call the police! Get us out of here!" Dash demanded.

George moved to the second room on the left and saw the shadow of Pierre. He flung a grenade into the room and made a quick comment.

"*Au revoir* (Goodbye)" George said.

The grenade exploded and the sounds drowned out Pierre's screams. He was dead in less than thirty seconds.

Tex called the police and told them that George Lorin was shooting up the building and he had explosives. Tex grabbed a Colt

M4 semi-automatic rifle from the closet in Dash's office. He checked to make sure that he had a full clip of ammunition and a bullet in the chamber ready for firing.

Tex heard the explosion in the last room on the first floor and aimed his gun toward the staircase entrance, located next to the elevator. This was the only entrance to the second floor.

He saw from the LED light over the elevator door that the elevator was coming up.

"Dash," Tex called out. "He's coming up in the elevator!"

"Watch the staircase door!" Dash ordered. "It could be a trick." Dash remained in his office.

Tex was alternating the aim of his rifle between the elevator doors and the staircase door. The bell that announced the elevator rang and the doors opened. Sitting in the middle of the elevator floor was a grenade that had a green light flashing on it.

Tex did an abrupt about-face and began to run when George stepped out from inside the elevator, raised his machine gun, and opened fire on Tex. George's bullets propelled Tex forward as he slammed to the floor. George casually walked up to him and shot him once in the head to make sure he was dead.

The fires on the first floor were beginning to fill the rooms and hallways of the second floor with smoke. George turned back toward the elevator and he saw the flash of a shotgun muzzle explode.

There stood Dash with a Mossberg 590 Tactical shotgun. The blast hit George in the left shoulder, spinning him around on the way to the floor. Dash walked toward him slowly, pumping the gun once to expel the used shell and place the next shell into the chamber.

"Not bad for an old man," Dash shared with his French accent. "Maybe I should have blown your head off. I know you're not an old man, George. You wear a disguise well. The question I have for you is: Who are you?"

George's submachine gun was within reach, but George knew that Dash would not miss his target at this range. Attached to the end of his shirt sleeve was the detonator to remotely detonate the grenades. Dash leveled his shotgun to shoot George point blank in the head and George detonated the grenade that was in the elevator.

The building shook and Dash looked back momentarily to see what was happening. That was all the time it took for George to grab his submachine gun and open fire on Dash. The bullets pulverized his body and his blood could be seen damaging the fine fabric of his suit.

Dash's body was propelled to the ground, but he was not dead yet. Fire was enveloping the entire building and George wanted to leave him with one final comment.

"Thank you for the opportunity."

There were five grenades left and George placed them near Dash, just out of his reach. George walked through the fiery area near the elevator and down the staircase to the first floor. He made his way through the inferno and exited through the door he came in. He walked the same straight line through the parking lot and waited for a moment near the street.

As he stood there, he could hear sirens in the distance that were getting closer. A blue 1987 Chevy Nova pulled up alongside of him and the passenger window rolled down as it approached. Inside there were two white-haired people, a husband and a wife, both in excess of eighty-five years old, who looked lost.

"Excuse me, sir," the woman called to him. "Do you know how to get to St. Joseph's Church?"

George placed his right hand on the window ledge of the door and kept the machine gun behind him. Blood was dripping down his left arm from the area where he was shot by Dash. The people in the car didn't notice that the building was now fully engulfed in flames.

"Yeah. You go down this street, the street you're on, for about a-half mile and turn right onto West Pine Street. Stay on that for about a-half of a mile and make a left on North Lincoln Ave. About six blocks down, it'll be on your left."

"So, right, then left?" the old woman asked. George nodded. "Thank you so much."

The old people drove away. Smitty and Gar picked up George immediately for their return trip to Coeur d'Alene. As soon as George entered the van, he detonated the last five grenades.

Part 3

CHAPTER 42

Daisy Zacaro sat at her desk perusing an email from the FBI's Questioned Documents Unit. Daisy had sent the original signature page from the Loma National Bank, when a bank account was established in the name of a company called Copyization. The signatures on the document were for a woman named Rebecca Nguyen and Roger Legion.

Daisy's blood pressure continued to escalate as she read the report that accompanied the email. It concluded that Rebecca Nguyen's signature was authentic, but Roger Legion's was not original. It was deemed a forgery.

"God damn it!" she uttered aloud in her empty office and thought about breaking something. She quickly reconsidered.

She picked up the phone and dialed the author of the report.

"Questioned Documents, Meredith speaking," a voice answered."

"Hello, Meredith. This is Daisy Zacaro, in the San Diego AGs office. How are you?"

"Fine, Ms. Zacaro. I suspect that you're calling me about the Copyization report?"

"That's right. I wanted to know if your findings were reviewed by anyone else in your office?" she quizzed.

"That's standard protocol," Meredith acknowledged. "We try to put two sets of eyes on everything."

"Who was the other person who looked at it besides you?"

"It was Cindy Bertram."

"I want Harry Van Slyke to look at it," she said stridently. "He's the best in my opinion."

"I don't know if that's possible. Harry's really backed up with work."

"I'm not asking you or anybody," Daisy conveyed. "You do it immediately or I'll have someone from the Attorney General's office in the Justice Department give you a call with the order. You understand?"

"Miss Zacaro," Meredith commenced, "this is a pretty simple open and shut case. The signature for Roger Legion did not contain live ink and if you look at his signature closely, it was cropped out of another document. At the bottom of the 'g' in the word, Legion, a very slight portion of it is sliced off."

"May I ask what your credentials are?" she asked in a callous tone.

"I have a Masters in Forensic Science from George Washington University," she relayed.

"Have you ever been a professor or published papers on the topic?"

"No," she answered.

"I'm done talking to you."

With that, she immediately slammed the phone back into its cradle. Her anger left her amped up and she stared at her desktop contemplating her next move. She picked up the phone and dialed a number. It was answered on the second ring.

"Chrisman," the voice answered.

The voice belonged to Special Agent Pete Chrisman. He was one of the agents who had Roger Legion under surveillance.

"This is Zacaro. The surveillance of Legion is back on. Get out there with your girlfriend partner. Let Legion know you're there. Squeeze him. And I expect daily reports."

Daisy Zacaro was not going to allow anything, including the facts, to derail her mission.

CHAPTER 43

Dusk was turning into night as FBI Special Agents Brenda Tomaras and Sam Mezner traveled from the armored truck crime scene, near Athol, Idaho up Highway 95 to Sandpoint. They had also stopped to inspect the wreckage from the Idaho State Trooper police cruiser that was destroyed when it was struck by a rocket-propelled grenade.

Sam drove the white, late model, Ford Explorer SUV, while Brenda continued an extended conversation with the FBI Special Agent-in-Charge of the Coeur d'Alene office and one of the Assistant Special Agents-in-Charge of the Salt Lake City Division Office of the FBI.

"All right," she said. "Thank you. I'll keep you advised."

With that the call ended. Brenda had information to share with Sam.

"They want to set up a task force and put at least a dozen agents on it. They already have people looking for a rental truck that may have lost a reflector lens."

At the initial crime scene, the FBI agents found a circular reflector cap that appeared to have fallen off the truck used by the thieves.

"You going to run it?" Sam asked.

"Yeah. As long as I don't screw it up."

"Don't talk like that, Brenda. If the Bureau had any doubt in your ability, they would have pulled somebody off another case."

"I don't know, Sam. I don't have a grasp on what we're dealing with here. The two State Troopers. The armored truck guards. And God knows what we're going to find up here at this building in Sandpoint."

"What are we going to look at?" Sam wondered.

"The Coeur d'Alene police said that when they went to question the management people at Parapet Logistics, one of the owners was real antsy. He told them to go talk to a guy named Henri Charlemagne in Sandpoint. This guy is a haberdasher. Makes clothes." Brenda stopped for a moment to look at a text on her phone. "Well, Henri's Haberdashery burned down today. They're sifting through the ruble right now and they found one body so far. What's more interesting is that the 9-1-1 system in Sandpoint received a call from Henri's Haberdashery today telling them that a guy named George Lorin was there shooting up the place and setting off explosives."

"Did they say how much was on the truck?"

"They don't have an exact number, however, it's believed to be in excess of five million dollars," she disclosed.

"So, I guess you don't think it's some homegrown, good-old-boy?" Sam inquired with a smile.

"With this body count, I sense we are going to confront something or someone very evil."

"Maybe, we find George Lorin and call it a day?" Sam quizzed hopefully.

"Maybe," Brenda answered, knowing that a crime of this magnitude would never be that easy to solve.

CHAPTER 44

It had been less than a week since the murder of San Diego Police Detective Peter Atherton in the elevator after his visit to Legion & Associates. Roger Legion was forced to deal with the police, the press, and sightseers with a morbid curiosity.

The police continued to press Legion on the reason why the man, who posed as murdered attorney, Rike Hessler, was at Legion & Associates. Roger was unable to answer that question, based on pure and simple attorney-client privilege. Some press outlets felt that Roger was hiding something, and in fact, he was.

Roger spent the morning returning phone calls on his 'number 24' line that was specifically established to avoid wiretap interference. Roger would occasionally have his secretary call someone on his behalf and then transfer the call to him. He would also have her schedule a certain time for him to make or return phone calls.

He placed a call to Veronica Bonner, a forensic image specialist, who was a former member of the FBIs Forensic Imaging Unit. She was in charge of their Forensic Photographic Studio, which provided support to the FBIs Laboratory Division and field offices for all evidentiary photography.

"Hello, Roger," Veronica answered with a tone of optimism.

"Ronnie, how are you?" he replied, trying to match her spirit.

"I'm fine. I'm keeping busy, but I've always got time for you. What's up?"

"I've got a photograph that I need you to review," Roger told her. "It's just one photo. All I need to know is if it is legit."

"Is it digital or do you know the speed of the camera?" she wondered.

"It's not digital and I don't know the speed. I would guess it's thirty-five millimeter."

"Send it over and I'll let you know," Veronica told him.

"Listen, Ronnie, do you think you can move this to the front of the line?"

"I can for you, Roger. Can you give me forty-eight hours?"

"That's perfect. I'll send one of our runners over with it. It will be in a plain white envelope with my name on it."

"Okay. I'll be looking for it."

"Thanks, a lot, Ronnie. You're the best," Legion told her and ended the call.

As he was placing the telephone receiver onto its cradle, one of the lawyers, Ned Chandler, stood in his office doorway, waiting for Roger to conclude his call. As soon as Legion caught sight of him, he waved him over to the desk.

Ned and Brian Stensler, another Legion attorney, were the architects of a scheme to rip off an insurance company by sending them bogus bills from a photocopy services company called Copyization.

"Come on in. Sit."

Ned began to speak as he walked over to a chair across from Legion.

"I got a call from the plaintiff attorney for that *Mackenzie* case. The one where Ogilvie wanted to sanction Brian."

Ned was referencing the case that Judge Harrison Ogilvie attempted to entrap Roger into making comments about illegal activity involving a mediation service, called Vici Resolutions.

"What's he want?" Legion asked, in his no-nonsense style.

"They want to talk settlement. But he'll only do it with you," Ned told him and awaited a response. Legion continued to stare at Ned. "What do you want to do?" Ned asked.

"I don't want you to call him back. He wants something from you. So, let him come and get it. When he gets you on the phone, I want you to tell him this, word-for-word." Legion paused for a moment. "'I'll see you in court,' then slam the phone down on him."

Ned looked at him and wondered about this tactic.

"I don't know, Roger. He's got a good case," Ned advised. "I thought you wanted to shut this one down?"

"If he's got such a good case, why does he want to settle it? I will shut it down, but not until he spends more money. I don't want him to bleed, I want him to hemorrhage. He needs to realize the cost, figuratively and financially, when you come up against Legion & Associates. You understand?"

"Yes," Ned answered without emotion. He nodded and rose, heading to exit.

"Ned," Roger called out to him. Ned stopped to look back at him. "Don't ever tell me how strong a plaintiff's case is. That's their job and it implies our case is weak. If we go to trial, I will get a defense verdict. The plaintiff attorney knows it. And he's afraid. His fear is what we need to capitalize on. Regardless of the facts, his fear makes his case weak. And he knows it."

Ned again started to leave.

"You've got to learn these things, Ned," Roger pontificated. "You've got to decide if you want to try cases or sit on the sidelines and watch others do it."

Ned acknowledged his comment and walked out the door directly to his office. He wondered if he had just been in the presence of a great lawyer or a man in need of psychiatric intervention.

CHAPTER 45

At 7:30 am, on this Sunday morning in the Coeur d'Alene field office of the FBI, eight agents assembled for a briefing by Special Agent Brenda Tomaras on the status of the Sandpoint armored truck heist. This was the first meeting of the task force set up to find the perpetrators of the deadly robbery.

Brenda wore blue, straight-leg pants, with a white, button shirt and a gray blazer. The blazer was large enough to allow her to carry a shoulder holster for her Smith & Wesson M & P .40 caliber semi-automatic pistol.

The men, seated around the conference room table, all wore white, button shirts, either long sleeve or short sleeve. None of them wore sport coats. In addition, each wore a conservative tie. The men also wore either a shoulder or waistband holster to accommodate their weapon.

The conference room where the meeting was being held was bland, with a picture of the President and the Director of the FBI at one end of the room and an American flag at the other. In the center of the room was a conference table and every agent had a cup of coffee that accompanied where they sat.

"Our perpetrators," Brenda commenced, "took down the Mondo Run. For those of you who don't know what that is, it is one of the largest cash hauls made by an armored truck company during the year. It appears these people had access to the trip tickets. Our information is that one of the owners of the armored truck company, along with a guy named Henri Charlemagne, goes by 'Dash,' a haberdasher in Sandpoint, hired a guy named George Lorin to pull off the heist. The real plan of Dash and the owner was to double-cross Lorin, while they made off with the cash from the Mondo Run. Lorin found out about it, found the right armored truck and went on a killing spree. Two troopers who were escorting the truck were killed by a rocket-propelled grenade. The three crew members of the armored truck were killed by what appears to be a powerful and technically advanced grenade."

"Do we have any intel on people using these types of weapons and explosives in this area?" one of the agents asked.

"We haven't found anything yet," Brenda replied. "We're looking at some local militia groups, but I think this weaponry is too sophisticated."

"It's has to come from some place closer to the coast. We have to look at Washington and Oregon. Maybe even California," another agent shared.

"The remnants have been sent to the Hazardous Devices Operations Center in Quantico," Brenda continued. "They are going to make this a priority. Just to finish with the facts, as known, after Mr. Lorin and his crew get the cash, they travel back to Sandpoint to Dash's office, which is a small warehouse building, where they kill Dash, two of his employees and burn down the building."

"Excuse me, Sparkplug, but any video from Sandpoint?" an agent asked.

"I'm not fond of that nickname," Brenda shared with a daggered glance. "But to answer your question: Nothing yet. We believe we have either Lorin or somebody from his crew's DNA. There was a trail of blood coming out of the building that ended at the street."

Brenda stopped for a moment and looked around at the men.

"The other four members of our task force are out right now looking for a rental truck that lost a reflective lens, which Sam and I found at the crime scene."

As she finished her sentence, her cell phone chime filled the air. She stared for a moment at the Caller ID.

"It's one of our guys." She pushed a button on the phone to answer the call.

"Tomaras." A brief moment passed. "Where?" Another moment passed. "What's the name on the rental agreement?" A third moment. "Get a copy of the rental agreement. Find out if he has a storage unit there."

The information put Brenda into deep thought.

"They just found the truck," Brenda announced to the group. "It's at the U-Haul place on West Seltice Way."

"That can't be more than a-half mile from here," one of the agents shared.

"What's the name on the rental agreement?" another agent quizzed.

"George Lorin," Brenda responded in a deadpan tone. "I want two of you guys to get out there. See what leads come from it. Sam," Brenda said, referring to her partner, "you continue to see what you can find on the name George Lorin. I want two people at Parapet Logistics and two in Sandpoint to see what you can find out about this guy, Dash, and how he found George Lorin." Brenda looked around the room. "Let's get going."

The men scrambled out of their chairs to commence their assignments. Brenda's partner, Sam, had a comment to share with her.

"There's a lot here, Brenda. We'll get these guys."

"That's what bothers me," she replied introspectively. "There's too much. We could walk to that U-Haul place. George Lorin wanted us to find that truck. I think he wants to play a game with us."

Brenda had no idea how deadly of a game it was about to become.

CHAPTER 46

Detective Margaret Byrne sat in the last pew of Saint Joseph's Cathedral, located on Third Avenue in downtown San Diego, following the conclusion of the daily noon-hour Mass. Her goal was to attend Mass daily, when her schedule allowed, but now she made it the focus of her day, since the murder of her partner, Peter Atherton.

Margaret wore a floral print dress that she purchased at Macy's and a white kerchief over her head. Her Sig Sauer semi-automatic .9 millimeter pistol sat in her purse.

Detective Atherton was buried with full honors and Margaret was placed on two weeks of administrative leave, with pay. Following San Diego Police Department policy, she was taken off the case to find the killer of attorney, Rike Hessler, and she believed, even though it was never said, that every police officer blamed her for Pete Atherton's murder.

Margaret wanted to assist the current detectives investigating Pete Atherton's killing, but they politely refused. Margaret did not blame them. She felt responsible for her partner's death. When she saw his three children, sitting next to their mother,

Pete's widow, to accept a flag from the Honor Guard, she would have done anything to change places with Pete.

Margaret wanted to do something, but felt powerless. She tried to find the answers with God, but she knew that the only person who could help her find the answers was Roger Legion.

CHAPTER 47

Special Agent Brenda Tomaras arrived at the U-Haul Moving & Storage on West Seltice Way shortly after 8:30 am to determine what evidentiary information from the truck used in the robbery was available. She was met by the manager of the facility and Tom Bittner, an FBI Special Agent assigned to the task force.

"What do we have?" Brenda asked, with no-nonsense zeal.

"Driver's license, credit card, and the rental agreement," Agent Bittner declared. "All link back to George Lorin."

"Did you run the driver's license through DMV?" she inquired.

"There was no hit. It's a fake," the Agent told her.

"Let's run the picture for a facial recognition scan. Did he have a storage unit here?" she inquired of the facility manager.

"Yeah. I can show you where it is," the manager answered.

"We'll get a search warrant," Brenda shared.

"No need," Agent Bittner replied. "They left it opened. It was cleared out. Crime scene technicians are on their way."

Brenda looked down at the ground and rubbed her forehead in an attempt to fend off an oncoming headache.

"Where's the truck?" she inquired.

The three of them walked across the parking lot to see the ten-foot box truck sitting like a lonely sentinel. As she neared the truck, Brenda donned a pair of green latex gloves.

"How many people have touched this truck since it was returned?" Brenda asked the manager.

"Just one guy," the manager answered. "Name's Luco. He drove it from the entrance over here and checked the gas. He was supposed to wash it, but it was late. He was going to do it today, but then you guys showed up."

Brenda walked up to the passenger door of the GMC truck and opened it.

"What are you doing?" Agent Bittner asked, somewhat shocked because she may be tampering with fingerprint evidence.

Brenda reached into the truck and opened the glovebox as she answered him.

"I'm getting our next clue."

Within the glovebox was a small owner's manual. Rising from between the pages was a small piece of lined paper that Brenda removed. She looked at it and read it in front of the other two men.

"Meet at Gar's. Saturday – 9:30 pm. Smitty, Rollo & Floyd will bring Mondo to carve."

These were the men who assisted George Lorin with the Mondo Run heist. Next to Gar's name was his address on Hazel Avenue in Coeur d'Alene.

Brenda looked at Agent Bittner in disgust. She then posed a rhetorical question.

"Doesn't every thief write down information like this and leave it in their getaway vehicle?"

"Maybe we're just getting lucky?" Agent Bittner wondered.

"Maybe we're just getting duped?" Brenda retorted.

She handed the piece of paper to Agent Bittner and began the walk back to her car. At present, she had no choice but to play the game on George Lorin's terms.

CHAPTER 48

Terrance Haden, the United States Attorney for the Southern District of California, stood in the doorway of Daisy Zacaro's office waiting for her to conclude a telephone call. Terry stood six feet two inches tall, and weighed 175 pounds. He wore a white shirt with the sleeves rolled up halfway on his forearms and his yellow and blue stripped tie was loose around his neck. The top button of his shirt was unbuttoned.

Before Daisy was able to dial another number, he caught her attention.

"Daisy." She quickly gave him her attention. "Can I see you in my office?"

She followed him down the hallway. Terry's office was large and well appointed. He had a view of the ocean. His walls were covered with awards, photos with dignitaries and his family. As soon as they both entered, Terry began.

"Shut the door." She complied. "Have a seat." Terry sat at his desk, while Daisy sat across from him in one of the two empty chairs.

"I just received a call from the FBI's Questioned Documents Unit," Terry advised. "You know that the one thing that we do not do here is shoot the messenger."

"I want to make sure that the messenger is competent enough to deliver the message," she replied.

"Well," Terry retorted without emotion, "you're going to have to live with the report they produced. I'm sorry that Legion's name isn't on there, but the facts are what the facts are."

"Look Terry, I've got history with Harry Van Slyke. If he says it's not legit, I'll live with it."

"Daisy," Terry responded as his patience began to grow thin, "you are going to live with the original report they produced."

"Terry, I know he'll review it for me."

"I SAID NO!" he flared.

His booming voice resonated in his office. He stared at her for a moment.

"The last thing I want is for this office to be seen as a bunch of rogue attorneys, who think they're impervious unless they get what they want. The only way we are going to get things done is through cooperation. You either learn to work with others, or I don't want you working here." Terry paused for a moment. "Everything we do here is high profile and there are consequences for reckless action. Now, I don't want you making enemies. Understand?"

"Yes," Daisy answered as if she had just swallowed a bitter pill.

"I think we need to re-evaluate this Legion case," Terry told her. "It seems to me that someone must be setting him up."

"No," she said calmly shaking her head, "no, no. Roger Legion is a master manipulator. I suspect that in the overall plan, this situation with the signature was built-in, so we would stop looking in his direction. I'm on to his bullshit and he knows it."

"Daisy," Terry asserted and leaned toward her, "you've got to be able to prove it. Don't let your hatred of Legion blind you to the facts of the case. My suggestion in this instance, and I will memorialize it in a memo, is that we bring Legion in and offer him a deal."

"What kind of deal?" Daisy responded, incensed at the thought.

"Have him plead guilty to one count of wire fraud with any jail time being suspended. We'll detail the facts in a letter, send it to the State Bar and advise that, in our opinion, this was not a crime of moral turpitude, but rather, simple negligence. In exchange, we'll seek his assistance in finding out who, at his firm, is responsible for this crime."

"Terry," Daisy declared with a visage of flummox. "You're new to the area. You don't know Roger Legion. You try to pitch that to him and he is going to laugh right in your face. The guy has never lost at trial, so he thinks that he is going to skate on this. What we need to do is get him some bad press. That's what he fears. The insurance companies cutting him off."

"I don't like it," Terry maintained.

"After what happened in his office, where the cop got killed, Legion is a pariah. Let me turn up the heat, just a little, and he'll come to us. Just like he did the other day in our office."

Daisy referenced Roger Legion barging into their office demanding to know why his phones were tapped and he was being surveilled.

Terry peered at Daisy and let out a sigh as he ran his fingers through his hair.

"All right," Terry relented. "But if anything goes sideways, you're off the case and maybe even right out the door. You walk this trail alone. You take the praise and you take the blame."

Daisy rose from her chair.

"Yes, sir," she declared.

Daisy had a renewed vigor in the destruction of Legion & Associates. Her next step was to surreptitiously question several randomly selected Legion attorneys. One of the attorneys selected would be Brian Stensler, one of the planners of the fraudulent billing scheme.

CHAPTER 49

At approximately 9:25 pm, Special Agent Brenda Tomaras sat in her FBI-issued white, Ford Explorer, on Hazel Avenue in Coeur d'Alene, approximately one-and-a-half blocks from Gar's house on North Fifth Street. From her position, she could see the front door of the house.

Shortly after the note was found indicating that the loot from the Mondo Run heist was going to be divided up that evening and all the men would be in one location, Brenda ordered an FBI SWAT team to be mobilized to assist in the arrest of all of the thieves.

The SWAT team moved stealthily to take up positions that allowed them to have Gar's house totally surrounded. They evacuated residences that were adjacent and across the street from Gar's house. The Coeur d'Alene Police Department would be providing assistance by setting up a perimeter within one block around the house in the event anyone attempted to escape.

A command center was set up two blocks from Gar's house and the SWAT commander was in charge of the operation. Brenda listened to the radio chatter for information on all movement. The neighborhood was unusually quiet and the streetlights buzzed in the autumn night.

Earlier in the day, the FBI had identified the type of vehicle driven by Gar. It was a gray, Toyota Tundra with an extended cab. They had issued a BOLO or 'Be On the Look Out' for the truck to all police authorities in the area. The truck was located in the afternoon at a 7-Eleven convenience store, less than a mile from his house, where Gar worked part-time.

A voice on the police radio began the event.

"Suspect vehicle is in motion, heading north on Sixth Street passing East Spokane Avenue. Occupied four times."

The voice was indicating that there were four occupants in the vehicle.

"Suspect vehicle is now turning west on East Hazel. ETA (Estimated time of arrival) less than thirty seconds."

When Gar's truck turned the corner, it was right in front of Brenda's Ford Explorer. She could see in the bed of the truck a large, wooden container that was approximately three-feet wide, six-feet long, and four-feet high.

When the truck arrived, Gar raised the overhead door on his garage and backed in. As soon as the truck was in, the overhead door began to descend.

Inside the garage, Smitty, Floyd, Rollo and Gar removed the crate from the truck and set it on the garage floor.

"Where's George?" Floyd wondered.

Smitty took out his cell phone and called George on speed dial.

"Yeah," George answered.

"Where are you? We want to get going," Smitty told him.

"I think I got a cop on my tail," George responded with concern. "Give me a few minutes to lose him. Is everybody there?"

"We're here and ready to go."

"I'm on my way." With that George ended the call.

Brenda continued to surveil the house and the neighborhood, while listening to the SWAT Team conversation.

"There's only four of them. What do you want to do?" a voice asked.

"Let's give him a few more minutes."

In Brenda's passenger-side mirror, she caught a glimpse of a 2001 Dodge Ram 2500 4x4 that had its suspension raised. This caused the truck to sit approximately two feet off the ground. The front bumper was made of diamond patterned steel with a thick, metal grate to guard the front of the truck, known as a push bar. To Brenda, the truck simply appeared odd.

Brenda's cell phone then went off. She looked at the Caller ID. It was the SWAT commander.

"Tomaras," she answered.

"I just want to get your input on this. We can take the four right now. I have no idea who's missing. My concern is, if that overhead door goes up and they come out. I don't want to have a shootout on the street. What do you think?"

Brenda paused for a second.

"Execute the plan," she advised.

"Roger that," the SWAT commander told her and moved to the police radio.

"Entry teams. Prepare for entry. Don't move into place yet. Advise when flashbangs are ready to deploy. Snipers, advise what you got eyes on."

It was then that Brenda heard the diesel engine of the Dodge Ram 4x4 start and its high beam lights flood the area in front of it. It caused Brenda to squint to see what the truck was doing.

Then, she heard the SWAT commander's voice on the radio.

"Entry teams move into place."

As he finished that sentence, the garage erupted. The explosion was so powerful and so unexpected that it blew the four walls of the garage out and the roof pancaked down onto the floor of the garage. It unleashed a concussive power that took out all windows in the adjacent buildings and some nearby cars. Brenda's Ford Explorer shook as she ducked her head down to avoid any shrapnel.

The garage burned intensely as did Gar's house. The explosion blew SWAT team members off their feet as firetrucks and ambulances were immediately called.

Brenda saw the Dodge Ram pull a U-turn and she decided to take off after it. The Dodge traveled east on Hazel and turned south on to North Tenth Street. Brenda was now in a high speed pursuit. Due to the events at Gar's house, she refrained from calling anyone on the police radio. She hoped a police car would see her and get involved in the chase.

The Dodge now made its way to East Harrison Avenue and headed west at speeds in excess of seventy miles per hour. The truck was moving erratically, nearly missing vehicles and not paying attention to warning signs or traffic lights. Brenda was less than a-half mile behind the truck.

The Dodge then turned north on North Fifteenth Street with an open throttle. Brenda was having a tough time keeping pace with the vehicle as it turned east onto East Hazel Avenue. This portion of East Hazel Avenue was located on the other side of Highway 90.

Brenda lost sight of the Dodge, but saw where it turned. She made the turn at high speed and her Ford Explorer fishtailed into the street. She continued to follow the road in search of the Dodge truck.

When she reached East Skyline Drive, the road became more rural. There were no sidewalks and more trees surrounding occasional driveways. Brenda could see no vehicles in the distance and she slowed her pursuit to nearly a crawl, trying to scan the night view as best she could, utilizing her vehicle's headlights.

She passed three driveways and saw no movement. As she was passing the fourth driveway, on the driver's side of her vehicle, she heard the roar of the Dodge. Brenda only caught a flash of the truck before impact. It careened out of the driveway, with its gas pedal pressed against the floorboard, and t-boned the Ford Explorer.

The power of the collision smashed the glass windows on the driver's side of the vehicle as it lifted it up and flipped it off the road. In addition, the driver's side airbag deployed as the vehicle's driver's door was caving in on Brenda. This caused the airbag to tear her shirt and rip a portion of her skin off, while it filled with air.

The car rolled three times down an embankment before stopping on its roof. The violent hurling of the car pummeled Brenda's petite body. When it stopped, she was confused and dizzy. Hanging upside down by the vehicle's seatbelt, she saw the blood on the airbag. Brenda realized, from the pain in her chest, that she must have broken at least one rib. She slowly reached for her handgun, but it was gone.

The moonlight illuminated the area enough that she could see up a hill to her right. The road was at the top of the hill. Passing motorists would not see her vehicle until morning. She needed to find either her cell phone or the police radio.

Brenda struggled with her seat belt and forced it out of the clip. Her mangled body landed on the ceiling of the Explorer and she started to slowly look around through intense pain.

She stopped for a moment as she heard something outside the vehicle. It was the sound of footsteps crunching on fallen leaves. Brenda started to crawl out the driver's window and she stopped cold when she heard something.

It was the hammer on her Smith & Wesson M & P .40 caliber revolver being pulled back.

"Hey, Sparkplug. Do you know what that sound is?" The voice was cocky and self-assured. "That's the sound of futility. Like you trying to catch me. It can't be done. You know why? Because I'm smart and you're stupid. Now you forget about me and everything will be fine. Otherwise, I'm going to have to kill your husband and your daughter before I kill you. And I know your daughter really likes going to the bookstore with you."

Even though she had never heard his voice before, she knew it was George Lorin. He crouched down and pressed the barrel of the gun into her skull, right behind her left ear.

"Sparkplug," George spoke as the gun pressed her face into the dirt. "You know what they call a cop without a gun?" He paused for a moment. "Useless." He paused again. "You know what they call a female cop without a gun?" A third pause. "Very useless."

George stood up and lowered the hammer on the gun. He then tossed it approximately fifteen feet away. George backed up two feet from Brenda and kicked her in the head with his steel toe work boot.

Brenda went from having a concussion to being in a coma.

CHAPTER 50

A rare rain shower blanketed San Diego and Roger Legion took a moment from reviewing files in his office to observe the dark clouds gathering.

The Unibility Insurance audit was scheduled to commence in less than a week and he decided to review all of the requested files on his own. With all the activity involving the FBI, he was of the belief that there was no one at Legion & Associates that he could trust.

On the one hand, Roger thought that when the truth came out, he would be cleared of any wrongdoing. On the other hand, with Daisy Zacaro's seething hatred of him, she probably would not play with an honest deck. What he hated most was the potential negative publicity surrounding the entire matter. This, coupled with the recent events involving the murder of San Diego Police Detective Peter Atherton, would continue to keep Legion & Associates in the spotlight.

Roger Legion's cell phone sat on his desk set to vibrate. Roger's gaze at the dark clouds was broken by the sound of the vibration. He picked up the phone and saw, on the Caller ID, the name 'Acitu Insurance.'

"Roger Legion," he answered.

"Roger, it's Lisa Leffort. How're you doing?" she asked.

"I'm fine, Lisa. How are you?"

Lisa Leffort was the claims manager at the San Diego branch of Acitu Insurance. Acitu had been a client of Legion & Associates for many years and Lisa was always impressed with Roger's work.

"I'm good," Lisa replied. "I just wanted to let you know that the FBI went to our regional office in Sacramento asking questions about your billing. You got any idea why they're asking?"

"It's a long story, but the bottom line is that somebody hates me and is trying to cause trouble for me."

"Well, I got a call from our Vice-President of Claims. He said not to send you any more work until this situation is clarified."

Roger took a moment to digest Lisa's statement.

"All right," Roger told her. "I hope that maybe in a week or two, the whole situation will be clarified."

"Roger, I've got six files over here. You send a runner to come and pick them up. I'm going to say that I sent them to you before I had the conversation with our Vice-President."

"Thank you," Roger told her, truly grateful for her friendship. "I hope you know that I'm going to pay for your daughter to go to college."

"Wow," Lisa replied, not believing what he had just said.

On Roger's landline phone, a call was beeping for him and Lisa could hear it.

"You take that," she said referring to the other call, "and I'll be in touch."

"Thanks again, Lisa," he told her and ended the call. Roger then pushed the blinking button on the landline phone.

"Yes?" he inquired.

"Glenn Edgarian is on line six," Nina, the receptionist, told him. "He said he wanted to hold."

"Put him through," Legion told her.

The phone rang again and Legion answered it.

"Hello, Glenn," Roger said.

"Roger," Glenn began, his voice was hurried. "I've got something for you on Crazy Daisy, but I don't want to talk about it on the phone. When do you have time to get together?"

"This afternoon?" Roger suggested.

"I can't do it. I'm in North County. What about tomorrow?"

Roger quickly looked at his electronic calendar.

"How about ten o'clock?" Roger asked.

"I'll see you then," Glenn responded and ended the call.

As Glenn spoke the last sentence, Nina, the Legion & Associates receptionist, appeared in Roger's doorway.

"Nina, what's going on?" Legion wondered.

"Rike Hessler just called."

A pall enveloped the room. Roger knew this call was coming, but he had no idea when to expect it.

"Is he on the phone now?" Roger inquired in a rushed cadence.

"No," she replied. "He told me to bring you my cell phone and said for you to call him back on it at this number."

Nina handed her cell phone and a small piece of paper to Roger. Roger looked at the number and dialed it on her phone. Nina returned to her desk.

"Mr. Legion," the man claiming to be Rike Hessler answered with a proud German accent. "Your promptness is very much appreciated."

"Should I refer to you as Rike Hessler?" Legion asked.

"That's a detail that we can work out at a later time. Right now, I want to discuss the conclusion of our business."

"The photo that you gave me," Legion shared, "is being reviewed right now. I'll get a report on it tomorrow."

"Very good. Now what did you have in mind for the transfer of funds."

"Do you want cash, certified check, or a wire transfer?" Legion quizzed.

"I believe that a wire transfer would be most efficient."

"Get me the instructions and we'll set it up," Legion replied. "I have the funds now."

"Mr. Legion, your reputation is well-deserved. You'll receive the wire instructions closer to the actual time of transfer."

"I can tell you that I don't like having a reputation for having police officers murdered in the elevator of my office."

"That was most unfortunate and I can assure you, it was not what I had planned."

"Listen, Mr. Hessler, as I had told you, I will need you, or whoever you are working on behalf of, to come in here and sign a release and confidentiality agreement."

"You let me know when you are comfortable to transfer the funds. I will make an unannounced visit to your law firm and sign whatever you want me to sign, as soon as I am assured that the funds have been transferred."

"How do I contact you?" Legion queried.

"You don't. I will call your young lady and I will give her my number for you to call me. Understood?"

"Yes," Roger told him.

"Mr. Legion. Don't do anything foolish, like involve the police. As you know, that can have deadly consequences. *Auf Wiedersehen* (Goodbye.)"

The call ended and Roger was flustered. He rested his forehead in the palms of his hands, looking down on his desk, and thought about his options. Daisy Zacaro's plan was having its desired result. The potential loss of business was making Roger Legion squirm.

Roger grabbed Nina's cell phone and was going to walk down the hall to return it to her. It was then that an email, in Roger Legion's inbox from a former attorney named Michael Eiffert, caught his eye.

Meanwhile, at the federal office of the US Attorney for the Southern District, Daisy Zacaro's ringtone, which sounded like an old fashioned telephone, began to play. She looked at the Caller ID and answered it.

"Yeah," Daisy said without interest.

"He just got off the phone with Edgarian," the voice said. "Edgarian didn't tell him anything, but they're gonna meet tomorrow."

"You know what to do," she simply stated and ended the call.

On her desk was a newspaper photograph of Roger Legion. Daisy had doodled a noose around his neck and various knives sunk into his body. She had also drawn a cut-off penis falling from his body and blood spurting out of the location where it was cut off.

When she was done with her phone call, she refocused on her doodling.

CHAPTER 51

Glenn Edgarian emerged from the Starbucks Coffee Shop on El Camino Real in the Vons Shopping Center, shortly after 9:00 am, as he did nearly every weekday morning. Glenn would order a Grande Cafè Americano, which was the medium size, but ask for it in a Venti or large size cup. This would allow him to add sugar and milk to his liking and minimize the opportunity to spill it.

Glenn was fifty-eight years old, but with the body of a twenty-five year old. His 205 pounds on a six-foot-two-inch frame, appeared to be carved out of granite. If it wasn't for his gray hair, feathered back, you would easily believe that he was twenty-five years younger than his actual age. He wore a light blue Ralph Lauren Polo shirt, jeans, and cowboy boots.

He approached his 2008 GMC Denali SUV and used his pocket fob to unlock the doors. As he did, a voice called out to him.

"Excuse me, sir," a man in his early 30s, wearing a suit, requested his attention. Glenn stopped and looked at him with his trademark smile. "Do you know how to get to the 5 freeway from here?"

As Glenn began to give him directions, the man moved in front of Glenn, approximately three feet. From behind Glenn's vehicle, another man appeared and directly approached Glenn's back. The man had a Vipertek VTS989 stun gun and plunged it into Glenn's back as he pulled the trigger on it. This stun gun had the ability to deliver 38 million volts of electricity to the target.

As soon as Glenn felt something touch his back, he pivoted like a defensive lineman with his left elbow up. His elbow caught the head of the second assailant in mid-swing and smashed it into the door column of his SUV. As this was occurring, the first assailant also pulled out a stun gun and put it up against Glenn, giving him a full shock. His face grimaced and his body froze like a statue. He fell to the ground between two cars without moving either of his arms to break the fall.

The first man looked at the second man, who was trying to shake off the pain.

"You all right?" he asked.

"Yeah," he replied as he stood.

They both looked around while blocking any view of Glenn. The lot was still quiet.

"Pull the car around. Pop the trunk," the first man commanded and the second man complied. "You take his legs."

They picked Glenn up and put him in the trunk of their late-model Chevy Impala.

Glenn's meeting with Roger Legion would not take place this day. Crazy Daisy had other plans for him.

CHAPTER 52

Roger Legion walked out of the Hall of Justice after a quick status conference. As he waited for the light to change for the crosswalk on State Street, heading west, he heard a familiar voice.

"Hello, Roger."

He turned and saw San Diego Police Detective Margaret Byrne. Margaret wore a deep black, quilted fleece jacket, a light, yellow button shirt and stadium gray slim-leg ankle pants.

"Hello, Margaret," he acknowledged with a smile. "How are you?"

"All right," she replied, but he knew she was distressed.

They both crossed the street in the direction of the America's Finest City Building and Margaret wanted to share some information.

"You know you're being followed by two FBI agents?"

"I know," Roger replied with rather deadpan interest.

"Does it have anything to do with the murder of my partner?" she asked with heightened interest.

"Nope. It's a long story. Too long," he concluded.

"Have you heard from him?"

Roger Legion knew exactly to whom she was referring. She wanted to know if the man, impersonating Rike Hessler, had contacted him. He stopped to face her.

"Yes."

"And?" her voice oozed with anticipation.

"I'm still waiting on some information."

"You've got to let me know when he's coming," she begged and made it almost sound like an order.

"Look, Margaret, I don't know when he's coming. He told me it would be unannounced."

"Roger, I've got to stop this guy. I'm going crazy thinking about it."

"If I can call you, I will. But I'm not going to guarantee it," Roger sternly advised.

"If I can help you out with anything, let me know. These FBI guys, anything," Margaret said assuredly.

Roger looked at her and began to nod his head.

"Maybe there is something that you could help me out with?"

As he finished his sentence, he looked to Broadway, where he saw the FBI surveillance car passing by. FBI Special Agent Bob Malloy was driving and Agent Pete Chrisman was in the passenger seat.

As the car rolled by, Legion and Chrisman locked eyes and Chrisman nodded.

CHAPTER 53

On the twenty-fourth floor of the America's Finest City Building, a bell announced the arrival of an elevator car. The doors opened and Roger emerged, fresh from his visit to the courthouse and conversation with Detective Margaret Byrne.

Legion moved at a quick gait, walking directly to the receptionist's desk.

"Nina," he said and obtained her immediate attention. "Glenn Edgarian is coming in around ten o'clock. Send him back to my office, even if I'm on the phone."

Normally, a visitor to Legion & Associates would have an escort to proceed anywhere other than the nearby conference rooms. Glenn Edgarian was a frequent visitor to the law firm and therefore, allowed to go to the offices.

"Okay," she replied. "I have Veronica Bonner on the phone for you right now."

Veronica Bonner was the forensic image specialist that was reviewing the photo provided by the man claiming to be Rike Hessler.

"I'll take it in my office," he told her and moved swiftly to his corner office.

Roger picked up the phone before sitting down and pressed a button on the phone's base.

"Ronnie," he said. "Sorry for the delay, how are you?"

"I'm fine, Roger. How about you?"

"I'm good," he declared. "How's my photo?"

"Well, Roger," Ronnie began, "I had a chance to look at it and I can sum it up in three words: fake, phony, fraud."

"Really?" Roger answered with the wheels in his mind turning at high speed. "That's interesting."

"When the photo's enhanced," Ronnie disclosed, "you can see that the pixels don't line up correctly around the head of the guy in the picture. There are two distinct sizes of pixels and there should only be one. The cropping around the head on the picture is not as good as it could be, and finally, they tried to colorize it to give the photo the same tone. I was able to easily remove that."

"So, it's an amateur job?" Roger quizzed.

"Absolutely," Ronnie concurred. "It's probably somebody who thinks they're good with a photo manipulation program. And to the naked eye, it's not bad. But, like everything else, the devil is in the details."

"All right. Ronnie, you're the best. Email your bill over here today."

"Don't worry about it, Roger. It was pretty basic."

"No." Legion would not accept that response. "Send me a bill and include a rush charge."

"You know I want to keep you happy," Ronnie told him.

"Thanks again, Ronnie."

With that the call ended. Roger did not hang up the phone, but instead retrieved the business card of Keswick 'Kez' Thomkins, the general counsel for Zukunft and the man who hired Roger Legion to deal with the extortion attempt being made by the man

195

who killed Rike Hessler and San Diego Police Detective Peter Atherton. Legion dialed the number on his tap-proof line number twenty-four.

"Keswick Thomkins, please. This is Roger Legion."

Kez was on the phone within thirty seconds.

"Roger, how are you?" Kez queried, speaking fast. "Is it done?"

"No," Roger replied. "I just spoke with my forensic image expert. She says the picture's a fake."

"Yeah, so?" Kez demanded.

This was not the reaction Roger Legion expected.

"Kez, you've got nothing to worry about now. Your company is obviously the target of an extortionist and we can prove it."

"Roger, your direction from me was to pay the guy." The anger in his voice was distinct. "So, do what you're told and don't question me."

"Wait a minute, Kez," Roger began.

"No! It is in this company's best interest to have this matter go away quietly in the night," Ken lectured. "That's what I want. That is what I am telling you. Are we both speaking English?"

"Yes," Roger answered in disgust.

"Don't call me again until it's done," Kez demanded and hung up the phone.

Legion was perplexed. The thought of paying an extortionist sickened him. Now, he looked forward to the return of the man who killed a police detective in the elevator of his building.

Roger noticed the clock in the corner of his computer screen read 10:10 am. He wondered where Glenn Edgarian was.

Part 4

CHAPTER 54

At 6:10 am, the next morning, San Diego Police Detective Margaret Byrne drove a 2008 Chrysler 300 into the parking garage of the America's Finest City Building and proceeded three floors down to the lowest level of the garage. This level was nearly devoid of vehicles and Margaret drove up and parked adjacent to the elevators, with the engine running.

Within two minutes, she heard a rap on her trunk. She looked in the rear-view mirror and saw Roger Legion. Margaret popped the trunk and Legion got into it. Margaret left the building and drove to the Fashion Valley Mall in the Mission Valley section of San Diego. She found a desolate spot and Roger emerged from the trunk. He immediately took a position in the passenger seat.

"Is this your car?" he wondered.

"No, my neighbor's," Margaret shared. "I figured just in case the FBI are taking down the plate numbers, I didn't want it traced back to me."

"I really want to thank you for getting up so early to give me a lift," Roger told her.

"It's no problem. I try to stay close to your building, just in case he shows up." Her voice was sullen and detached.

"Are your people making any headway in finding out the guy's name?" Legion asked. "Because I don't know it. When he calls, he refers to himself as Rike Hessler."

"Does it deal with some kind of drug transaction?" Margaret inquired seriously.

"No," Roger answered as he shook his head. "I'm an insurance defense attorney. And it's got nothing to do with insurance or defense."

"I'm frustrated, Roger. They won't let me assist in the investigation. They won't tell me everything they know. They won't say it, but they think I violated procedure."

"Did you?" Legion responded, rather amazed.

"If Pete and I were both on that elevator, we would probably both be dead. We were set up to be ambushed."

"Why haven't they released a picture of the second guy? He's on video, right? They had a picture of the guy posing as Rike, and me, all over the paper, but I haven't seen the second guy."

"Good question. There is video from the elevator. I haven't seen it. I assume they don't want to spook him, so he feels free to move around."

Margaret and Roger continued north on the Interstate 5 freeway. Their destination was the McClellan-Palomar Airport in Carlsbad, California, approximately thirty miles from downtown San Diego.

After five minutes of silence, Roger had a question.

"Do you have any kids, Margaret?

"I've got two. A boy and a girl. One goes to Arizona State, the other works a minimum wage job. When my husband and I got divorced, they both wanted to live with him. So, I guess no 'Mother of the Year' awards for me."

"I would not draw any conclusions from a decision made by a child. Don't forget, I've seen you in action. I was in that room when all hell broke loose."

Roger was referring to the firefight that took place at Legion & Associates five years earlier. Margaret's partner was killed that day and she, along with a Legion lawyer, was able to stop the madness.

"Do you think about that day?"

"More than I should," Roger acknowledged gazing forward. He then turned to her. "You've got to stop blaming yourself. There's enough blame for everybody."

When they reached the airport, Margaret drove up to the hanger of a private plane terminal. Roger stepped out of the vehicle and turned back to her.

"Thanks again, Margaret," he told her with a smile.

"Call me when you get back," she said. "I can be here in thirty minutes."

"Okay," he acknowledged and entered the terminal.

Roger Legion was about to take an airplane ride and have a meeting with a person that he believed would be the solution to his FBI problem.

CHAPTER 55

In the intensive care unit of the Kootenai Health & Medical Center, located in Coeur d'Alene Idaho, FBI Special Agent Brenda Tomaras opened her eyes for the first time since being kicked in the head four days earlier. The first person she saw when she opened her eyes was her partner, Sam Mezner.

"Hey," she uttered with a gravelly voice. She had a shiny black eye from where she had been kicked in the face.

"Hey," Sam answered with a wide smile. "You done slacking off, because we've got to get back to work."

"How long have I been here?"

"This is your fourth day," Sam told her. "Your husband and daughter have been here the entire time. I just come over and relieve them, so they can go get a bite to eat."

"Tell me they caught George Lorin!" she demanded with rushed urgency.

"Not yet," Sam answered, as if he was ashamed of the response. "The task force is going full steam. Three shifts. Twenty-four hours a day."

"Who's in charge of it?" she wondered.

"Tom Bittner," Sam replied. "He knows what he's doing."

"The first good assignment I get and I lose it," Brenda commented with a tone of surrender. "I got to get back to the office."

"I wouldn't be in a hurry to go back. SLC (Salt Lake City) wants to know why you took off that night and never called for back-up or 9-1-1."

Salt Lake City was the location of the FBI Division Office that was in charge of the Coeur d'Alene satellite office.

"He timed it perfectly," Brenda maintained. "All the assets were headed to the explosion. I didn't think I could get anybody to help me."

"Well, if they thought it was George Lorin, I think you would have gotten some backup. Did he say anything to you out there?"

"He had my gun, pointed behind my left ear, pushing my head down. He told me not to try to solve the case because he's smart and I'm stupid." There was a moment of silence in the room. "Is his crew dead?"

"Well," Sam shared, "the four men in the house were killed. But you know what I find odd? This guy, George, is so kill-happy, why didn't he take you out when he had the chance?"

"He's not done using me," Brenda concluded. "He knew that his little speech would infuriate me. And I would stop at nothing until I caught him. What keeps me alive, partner, is the design of his plan."

Brenda's spot-on characterization of George Lorin's plan sent a shiver up both of their spines. Brenda wanted to get out of the hospital immediately. She had a killer to find.

CHAPTER 56

As a Gulfstream G450 private jet commenced its descent, its lone passenger looked out the window at the various shapes of parcels on the ground and wondered about the owners and the people who lived there. His focus was interrupted by the voice of a flight attendant.

"We'll be on the ground in twenty minutes, Mr. Legion."

"Thank you," Legion told her. The blonde, slender, young lady returned to her tasks in preparation for landing.

Legion looked around the cabin and he thought about all the hours that he billed insurance companies and what he had to do to get to this place in his life. He liked to think of his trial victories as wars and all the interactions with other attorneys were battles, or at least skirmishes. The one thing they all had in common was the blood loss, the dollars to be paid. Roger viewed his job as minimizing the blood loss.

Two hours later, inside the Five Loaves Coffee House, on Second Avenue in Great Falls, Montana, Roger Legion sat at a small, round table with a cup of coffee, served black, set before him. He leaned forward with his elbows on the table, his hands clasped, and turned to the person who joined him for coffee.

"I have a problem I think you can help me with," Legion told him.

His coffee partner also had a cup of coffee in front of him. He used a teaspoon to stir his coffee as Legion spoke. The stirring of the coffee and the sentence were complete at the same time. The man then tapped the spoon several times on the rim of the coffee cup. He wore a worn, blue, Dickies work shirt, with the same color pants, and black work boots. It was Michael Eiffert.

CHAPTER 57

Michael Eiffert was an attorney who worked at Legion & Associates for ten years and was a rising star. Five years earlier, in his last year there, he obtained three defense verdicts and, in Roger Legion's opinion, should have been named 'Attorney of the Year.'

Another attorney, named Ted Theopolis, talked Mike into assisting him with the robbery of a drug dealer. Their thought was to implement their skills as attorneys to a criminal enterprise. The two men stole eight hundred fifty thousand dollars in cash. At the same time, a Claims Manager from Acitu Insurance was murdered and the police looked at Mike as their prime suspect.

When the drug dealers who were robbed suspected Mike, it culminated in the firefight that took place in the conference room of Legion & Associates. Detective Margaret Byrne and her partner were there investigating the Claims Manager's murder. When it was all over, eleven people were dead and the ones left standing over the carnage were Margaret Byrne, Michael Eiffert, and Roger Legion. It was the firepower of Margaret Byrne and Michael Eiffert that actually stopped the madness.

The event disillusioned Mike on the practice of law and he decided to move, with his wife and daughter, to Great Falls, Montana, where he opened a gas station.

Great Falls was the home of Ted Theopolis, his co-conspirator and best friend, who was murdered by another attorney, named Mark Reynolds. Ted met his fate because he found out that Mark murdered the Claims Manager.

Over the years, Mike and Roger corresponded sporadically via email, but nothing ever in detail. When Roger was involved in a famous incident involving the Coronado Bay Bridge, Mike sent him a congratulatory email. Roger received an email from Mike just a few days earlier, when he last spoke with the man claiming to be Rike Hessler.

It was that email that planted the seed, which sprouted into Roger's unannounced trip to Great Falls, Montana.

At the Five Loaves Coffee House, Mike just stared at him, not believing that he was sitting across from Roger Legion. Legion's blue suit, with gray pinstripe, looked as if he had put it on minutes earlier. He appeared to be ready to walk into a courtroom.

"I have a problem I think you can help me with," Legion told him as he locked eyes with Mike.

Mike finished tapping his spoon on his cup and set it down.

"What kind of problem?" Mike wondered.

"I believe someone or someones have been sending out fabricated vendor bills. Now the FBI has a target on my back. The phones in the office are tapped. I'm under surveillance. And we're set to have a legal audit of our files from Unibility Insurance. I find out it's going to be done by undercover FBI agents."

"How the hell did this happen?" Mike asked. He was incredulous at Roger's revelations. "And how can they get a phone tap on a law firm?"

"To answer your second question," Roger began, "they would have never done it with a San Diego judge. They got a guy up in Orange County to sign the order. They're supposed to get off the phone if the call doesn't deal with the stuff they are looking for. You and I both know, they don't give a shit. I had my guy at the phone company put in a secure line."

As Roger spoke, Mike took a quick sip of coffee. He set the cup down as Roger finished speaking.

"What do you need from me, Roger?" Mike quizzed.

"I need you to come back to the firm, talk with the attorneys, and find out who is playing this manufactured billing game. This way I can get the FBI off my back, so I can concentrate on other things."

"Well, I know someone has been paying my bar dues for all these years. You know that you'd beat them in court?" Mike said with certainty.

"I know I would. My concern is that I don't want the insurance companies running for cover. That would have serious economic repercussions. And this woman attorney they have running the thing, she hates me. She wants to string me up. Toes up on a slab in the morgue."

"A skirt?" Mike was shocked. "Are you kidding? What's she so pissed off about?"

"I don't know. I've got Glenn Edgarian looking into it. So, what do you say?"

Mike stared at Roger, appearing to be in deep thought.

"Let me tell you something, Mike," Roger shared. "I think about that day in the conference room five years ago often. I think about you, and Ted, and Paul Clifford. And I think, these are men who listened to me, who learned from me, and they understood the practice of law. Because you can talk about civility all day long.

But in a courtroom, and when dealing with an adversary, you treat it like war, in a most brutal and savage sense. You and Paul Clifford were lawyers that day. I'm sure Ted was also."

"If you saw him in action, you would have been proud of him," Mike conveyed in a somber tone.

"That's why I'm here today. To get a lawyer to help me."

Mike again looked at Roger and realized that Roger always knew exactly what to say in any situation.

"I've been here a long time, Roger. I don't know."

"I don't want you to do it for nothing. You find whoever is responsible for putting the FBI on my back and I'll make it worth your while."

"What does that mean?" Mike replied.

"One million dollars, once the FBI is off my back," Roger told him.

Mike's reaction was muted. He sat back in his chair.

"I don't know, Roger."

"You gave up a lot more for less money five years ago," Roger stated in quick response.

"I think time does things to a man sometimes." Mike paused for a moment. "You know what I would be interested in?" Another pause. "A partnership in the law firm."

Now, it was Roger's turn to think.

"My experience is that law firm partnerships don't work. Somebody always wants to be the boss."

"That would be you. I could be your silent partner. Until you decide to retire. Are you planning on living forever?"

"You never know. A five percent partnership?" Roger quizzed.

"I was thinking ten," Mike retorted.

"Seven-and-a-half," Roger asserted decisively.

"You get the last word," Mike announced as he extended his hand to shake on the deal.

"When can you be in San Diego?" Roger inquired.

"I can be there Friday morning."

"All right," Roger acknowledged.

"Let me ask you something, Roger," Mike wondered. "What if I said, 'No'?"

"Then this would have been the most expensive cup of coffee I've ever had."

The comment brought a smile to both their faces. Roger Legion and Michael Eiffert accomplished what they wanted.

CHAPTER 58

Glenn Edgarian awoke with a skull-splitting headache and eyes that were unable to focus. For the last two days, he was placed in a drug-induced state, while being transported by his kidnappers.

He knew that the floor was sandy and gritty, and creepy, crawly bugs seemed to be everywhere. The smell of urine and feces permeated the air. Glenn rose from his stomach onto his knees and then to his feet. He soon realized that he was in a cell that appeared to be part of a jail. While his impaired vision was halting him from obtaining details, there were seven single person cells connected by a lone corridor.

The corridor had lights, along with some natural light poured in from small windows along the top of cement block walls.

Glenn wore contact lenses and he soon realized that his abductors had removed them.

"HEY!" he screamed out, leaning against the bars. "HELLO!" he again screamed trying to get someone's attention.

A door at the far end of the hallway from Glenn's cell opened and a Hispanic man, looking like some sort of law enforcement officer entered. He was forty-four years old, weighed nearly 300 pounds and was five feet eight inches tall. His gut hung well over his belt and his shirt appeared popped open at the widest point of his girth. He had black, wavy hair and scars on his cheeks from acne. His moustache was so bushy that it appeared fake. His gait was more like a waddle. In a shoulder holster, he carried a .44 caliber Smith & Wesson Model 29 with an eight-inch barrel. This was the same gun used by "Dirty" Harry in the movies.

Glenn continued to scream after the man entered the corridor.

"Hey, keep it down over there!" the man yelled out without a discernable accent.

Glenn stopped yelling when he heard the voice.

"Listen," Glenn started to speak before the man reached his cell. "You've got to help me. This is a mistake. What day is it?"

"Thursday," the man replied.

Glenn was somewhat shocked at the passage of time.

"Some guys grabbed me in Encinitas two days ago. The police are probably looking for me."

"Where's Encinitas? You mean Ensenada?" the man asked as he arrived just outside of his cell.

Glenn looked at the man because he was concerned about the question.

"No. Encinitas. Northern San Diego County," Glenn responded.

"You're a long way from home."

"Where is this place?" Glenn asked

"Santa Isabella in Chihuahua," the man shared.

Glenn began to rub his forehead in his attempt to comprehend the situation.

"Listen," Glenn told him. "Let me just make a call or two. I can straighten the whole thing out.

The man gazed at Glenn up-and-down, but Glenn was unable to put the man in sharp focus.

"What's your name?" the man asked.

"Glenn Edgarian."

"Well, Glenn, you're here waiting for the prison transport to take you to a Federal prison just outside Mexico City. They told me you signed a confession that you're a drug smuggler and they sentenced you to twenty-two years."

"I'm being set-up! Let me talk to someone in the American Consulate," Glenn pleaded.

"It don't work down here like they do it on TV or in the movies," the man told him. "You should have pleaded your case before you signed the confession."

"I was drugged!" Glenn blurted out, fueled by frustration.

"Take it easy," the man advised. "You want to get out of here?"

"Yeah," Glenn answered in a serious tone.

"I need fifteen thousand dollars. Get somebody to wire it to you and I'll let you go."

Glenn looked at the man with an angry glare in forced surrender.

"All right," Glenn acknowledged. "Let me make a call."

"You gotta understand a few things, first," the man began. "If I let you go, you're gonna walk right out the door. I'm not going to help you get to the border or cross the border. You don't have a passport or driver's license, so I don't know how you're gonna do it. The prison transport comes every other day and they came yesterday, so the clock is ticking. *¿Comprender?* (Understand?)"

"I understand," Glenn told him. "What's your name?"

"Luz," he replied.

Luz reached into his shirt pocket and retrieved a cellular phone.

"So, you're Chief Luz?" Glenn wondered.

"Don't worry about my name. Worry about getting the money here on time. And no pissing in the corners. Use your bucket as a chamber pot." Luz stared at Glenn. "From this point forward, '*no hablo ingles.*' (I no speak English.)

Glenn was familiar with stories of corruption among the various officials south of the border. Even with his obscured vision, he was very clear on what had to be done.

CHAPTER 59

Daisy Zacaro sat at her desk reviewing daily reports regarding the surveillance of Roger Legion prepared by Special Agents Bob Malloy and Pete Chrisman. The more Daisy reviewed, the more agitated she became. Day after day appeared to be identical, as if they simply cut and pasted one day into the next.

It was then that the office intercom came to life.

"Yes," she answered with a petulant, perturbed tone.

"Agents Malloy and Chrisman are here," responded the voice.

"Send them back," Daisy answered and proceeded to collect all the daily reports into one pile.

Then there was a quick knock on the door and the two agents stood in the doorway.

"Come on in. Shut the door." Daisy's voice was civil, but an earthquake could await just under the surface.

The two men did as instructed.

"Have a seat," Daisy offered.

"If you don't mind," Bob replied, "we'll stand. We've been doing a lot of sitting lately."

Daisy nodded at his comment and the men stood at attention looking down at her.

"I was looking over your daily reports." Her words were slow and meted. "Not much going on with Roger Legion, huh?"

"No, ma'am," Pete responded.

"So, he just comes to the office, parks the car, and doesn't leave. Is that it?" Daisy wondered.

"That's pretty much the routine," Bob agreed.

"So, that's what he did yesterday?" Daisy quizzed.

"If that's what it says in the daily report, ma'am," Pete answered defensively.

"What if I was to tell you that Roger Legion took a private plane ride yesterday to Great Falls, Montana?"

Daisy simply stared at the men.

"I'd find that hard to believe," Bob replied.

"You know what I find hard to believe?" She began to stand as she continued to speak. "That the Federal Bureau of Investigation would ever have allowed TWO SHITHEADS TO BECOME SPECIAL AGENTS!"

The men stared at her with an icy glare.

"Are you guys stupid or lazy? Legion was able to give you the slip twice in the same day. YOU ASSHOLES SHOULDN'T EVEN BE CROSSING GUARDS!" Daisy spewed with histrionic flare.

"Can I inquire as to the source of your intel?" Pete demanded.

"Somebody from my office was at the airport in Carlsbad. They saw Legion there. You want to see a picture?"

A moment passed.

"No," Bob replied succinctly.

"When this debacle is over, I am going to make a recommendation to Quantico and I am going to make sure that every one of your missteps makes it into your jacket. And I am going to make sure that you are adequately compensated for your incompetence! NOW, GET OUT!"

The jacket she referred to was the Special Agent's personnel file.

The men exited the room and commenced a hurried saunter directly to the elevator. Not a word was spoken until the elevator doors closed.

"You think I could take her in a fight?" Bob asked, mimicking a question Pete had asked him during an elevator ride.

"Hell, yes!" Pete replied immediately. "That bitch is all bark. And she's one nasty lookin' ho."

"I love when you talk ghetto," Bob told him trying to keep a straight face.

"I love when you say stupid things, you racist bastard," Pete shared.

Bob held out his fist for a bump with Pete.

CHAPTER 60

Friday morning arrived and, as was the usual custom, Roger Legion began the attorney meeting with his usual gusto and bravado.

"Gentlemen," Roger began as he eagle-eyed each man in the room. "We welcome back a friend today, who has been gone for too long. Just before his departure, he had obtained three defense verdicts in a little over half a year. He is truly a utility man, able to handle anything in all instances. Some of you know him and the others will get to know him very soon. For now, I want him to oversee anything going to trial in the next ninety days, while he builds up a caseload. I present," as he pointed his open hand to him, "Michael Eiffert."

A round of applause filled the air and Roger wore a big smile, thinking what he had delivered. Mike rose to his feet to address the lawyers.

He wore a black Stefano Ricco Ricci suit with a white shirt and a diamond-patterned, yellow, silk tie. Mike's shoes were Florshiem black wingtips.

"I hope that I can shake off whatever rust I have on me quite quickly and begin doing what this law firm does best. We have a reputation for more than just excellent legal work. We treat adversaries as what they are: enemies that must be annihilated. Anything that gets in your way can be removed. You just have to know how to do it. A great man once told me that no one stands alone at this firm. So, whatever action you take, you have an army behind you. Right or wrong, you have the power to strike down the insidious foes, who seek to destroy us. Our ability to intimidate gives us the edge, regardless of the fact pattern. You've got to decide whether you want to shake hands with an enemy or strike them down. To help them up or render them impotent, paralyzed, and ineffective. If you want to shake their hands, then you're a traitor to this firm. And I would ask you to get out of this room right now. If you are dedicated to being a Legion lawyer, I'm going to help you with that journey. Now, let's go sharpen our knives."

Most of the attorneys in the room were amazed at how closely his speech mimicked a typical Roger Legion oration. The knife comment was identical. Roger Legion beamed with pride as his disciple spread his word.

"Listen to him, boys," Roger told them. "This is what I want you to become. Follow his example. He knows what he is talking about."

CHAPTER 61

As the afternoon was waning, Judge Harrison Ogilvie sat in his chambers and stared at a telephone message from US Assistant Attorney General Daisy Zacaro. He thought that he may be able to blackmail her with information he had gleaned regarding her connection to the Legion law firm. Before he went down that road, he wanted one more chance to snare Roger Legion.

From his desk drawer, he removed his Lanier P-164 micro-cassette recorder. Technology had advanced to the point where cassettes were no longer required in voice recorders, but the Judge could not recall the last time he used his recorder for official business. He preferred to use it on social occasions with some of his male visitors who liked to get 'silly.' The recorder had the ability to alter the speed of a voice, which most of his guests found hilarious.

The device also had a Voice Operated Recording (VOR) feature, which allowed it to record only when someone was talking or there was noise in the background. The Judge would sometimes set it to VOR to record the voices and breathing of his boyfriends during various sexual encounters, so he would have a souvenir of his conquest.

Judge Ogilvie picked up his telephone receiver and dialed two numbers.

"Yes," a voice answered.

"Edna, would you bring me two triple 'A' batteries?" he asked.

"Right away," she answered.

Within two minutes, the Judge's bailiff, who was built like a football player, named Bobby, knocked on the door and entered the room with the batteries.

"Can you get this going for me?" he asked the bailiff and handed him the recorder.

Bobby quickly removed the old batteries and inserted new ones. As soon as he closed the door on the battery compartment of the device, the recorder came to life.

The voice that they heard sounded familiar, but it was not the Judge, nor was it any of his social guests.

"You recognize that voice?" the Judge quizzed Bobby.

"Yeah," Bobby answered as a moment of realization arrived. "It's Roger Legion."

"You're right," the Judge concurred.

As they both continued to listen, Roger Legion described how Vici Resolutions, the mediation firm surreptitiously owned by Legion, was set up. He detailed different bribe methods that he used to persuade judges, which judges had partaken, and which judges he had on a 'leash,' who would never rule against him because it would threaten their ability to join Vici.

Apparently, the Judge was unaware that he had the recorder with him, the last time Roger Legion was able to get him out of jail. The recorder was set to the VOR or voice operated recording mode, so the conversation recorded without either person knowing that their every word they uttered was being captured.

The Judge looked at his bailiff with a wide grin.

"Bobby, I should buy a lottery ticket today," the Judge proclaimed. "That's all for now."

Judge Ogilvie picked up the receiver of his landline phone and furiously dialed Daisy Zacaro's cellphone. Her voicemail answered.

"Daisy," the Judge uttered with glee. "I got him. I got Roger Legion on tape detailing all the background on Vici Resolutions. He says who's involved and he says who's currently on the take. I'm leaving here right now, but I'll bring it to you first thing in the morning."

The Judge stood from his chair and retrieved his sport coat. He now had something to celebrate. He again dialed two numbers on the phone.

"Edna, I'm going home for the day. See you tomorrow."

"Okay," she replied.

Less than five minutes after the Judge left, Edna packed her bags for the day.

"See you tomorrow, Bobby," she said as she exited the courtroom.

"See ya, Edna," the bailiff told her.

Less than two minutes after she left, Bobby was on the phone.

"Legion & Associates," Nina answered.

"May I speak to Mr. Legion? My name is Bobby Colson. I'm the bailiff in Judge Ogilvie's department."

In Roger Legion's office, he was discussing recent case law with Mike Eiffert dealing with punitive damages and emotional distress, when the inter-office tone sounded.

"Yes," he answered.

"Bobby Colson is on line four," Nina told him. "He says he's the bailiff in Judge Ogilvie's department."

"Let me take this," he said to Mike. "Put him through," he told Nina.

The phone rang again and Roger picked up the receiver.

"Hello. This is Roger Legion."

"Hi, Mr. Legion. This is Bobby Colson from Judge Ogilvie's Department."

"Hi, Bobby, how are you?"

"I'm good. I just wanted to let you know something. Judge Ogilvie's got one of these old, handheld tape recorders that takes micro-cassettes. He asked me to put new batteries in it today. When I did, there was a tape in it that was a recording of your voice and the Judge talking about something called Vici Resolutions and a lot of other stuff. Well, the Judge was as giddy as a schoolgirl. I just wanted to let you know."

There was a moment of silence.

"Thank you, Bobby." Roger's voice was genuine. "I appreciate this. Did he say what he was going to do with that tape?"

"No."

"Can you do me a favor?"

"Yeah."

"Are you on your cell phone?"

"Yeah."

"Go into the Judge's chamber and press the redial button on the phone."

"Okay. Hold on," Bobby told him as he scurried into the Judge's chambers.

Bobby pressed the speaker button and then the redial button. After several rings, a voice that Roger Legion recognized answered. It was the voicemail of Crazy Daisy.

"This is Daisy, feel free not to leave a message."

"That help you out?" Bobby wondered.

"Yes, it does." A moment passed. "How's that new baby? I've got to send your wife something."

"That's not necessary, Mr. Legion. But, it's always appreciated."

"Don't worry. Thanks again, Bobby. We'll talk soon."

"Okay. Take care."

With that, the call ended. Roger Legion was in deep thought, gazing forward without focus until the voice of Michael Eiffert caused him to shift his attention.

"What was that?" Mike queried.

"A new problem," Roger shared in an emotionless voice.

"Let me handle it," Mike proposed.

Roger knew something had to be done. The question was: Which solution would be the best fit?

CHAPTER 62

When Special Agent Brenda Tomaras returned to work after four days in a coma and two days of observation and physical therapy, she received a less than hearty reception. While she was recuperating, Special Agent Tom Bittner assumed her position as head of the task force established to catch George Lorin, the presumed mastermind and perpetrator of the Mondo Run armored truck robbery and subsequent murders.

FBI agents were crisscrossing a three-state area following up on leads without much success. The only connection found to a previous crime was the use of a Confetti bomb in an attempted armored truck robbery outside Casper, Wyoming. In that instance, damage to the truck was so severe that the thieves had no time to empty the truck.

When Brenda entered the office, everyone was working diligently, saying 'Hello' and 'How are you doing?' but not much more. Her black eye was still visible, but not as shiny. She started to read some of the corkboard postings when she heard her name called out.

"Brenda," Tom Bittner exclaimed. "It's good to see you. Come on in my office."

Brenda followed him into his office and he closed the door.

"Have a seat," he offered and she complied.

"Are you close?" Brenda asked, demanded an answer.

"What? To catching Lorin?" A moment passed. "No," he answered succinctly.

"What about the truck? The jacked up Dodge Ram. There can't be that many of those out there." Brenda's impatience was evident.

"There are several thousand in the three-state area," Tom disclosed. "We've got BOLO's (Be On the Look Out) out there, so every law enforcement official is looking for that truck. We tried to conduct a facial recognition scan on the driver's license photo that Lorin provided to the rental company. The problem is that the picture was digitally manipulated. We have no fingerprints. We think we have his blood, but no DNA match. I don't like to say it, but this guy is good."

"He's gonna come looking for me," Brenda proclaimed. "He's not done with me yet."

"And that's a concern. As you might imagine, the brass down in Salt Lake City were quite upset when they found out that you took off after Mr. Lorin like a drunk cowboy when the law enforcement presence was overwhelming that night."

Brenda leaned forward in her chair.

"Tom, the house had just blown up. That's where the focus was. You know how fluid a stakeout is. You've got to make decisions fast."

"So, you take off like the Lone Ranger? Brenda," Tom retorted unapologetically, "he baited you and you took the bait. When you play the game his way, that's how you get killed."

"Tom, that's all we've been doing is playing the game his way. We've got to change it up."

"What do you suggest?" Tom replied rather sarcastically.

"Disinform. Leak something to the media that we've got him on video or we got a hit on the DNA. I'll do a press conference if you like."

"No." Tom was definite. "It would be one thing if we had the information and couldn't prove it. But we're flying blind here. And it's time that we all get to work. Now, Salt Lake City wants a statement from you detailing the events of that night and the reasons for your actions. I would prefer that they put you on a different case, but they said 'no' to that. So, after you finish your report, you are going to join your partner, Sam, and go through the tips from the tip line. See if anything sounds hot."

Brenda stood from her chair.

"Is that it?" Brenda asked with indignation.

"Brenda, if you want to take some vacation, just give the word. You deserve it. If you're going to be a drama queen, go do it someplace else."

"I'm telling you, Tom, Lorin is not done with me. If he was, you would probably be attending my funeral today. I'm not going to look for him. He's going to find me."

Brenda moved at a quick clip out of the office and left Tom's door open. Brenda's wisdom concerned Tom. If she was right, she was in danger. And Brenda's prophecy would soon bear fruit.

CHAPTER 63

Brian Stensler walked out of the North County Superior Courthouse, located in Vista, California, which is situated in the northern portion of San Diego County. He attended an afternoon settlement conference, but there was no settlement. It appeared that the case was now heading to trial.

Brian was accompanied by a claims representative from O-RISK-A National Insurance. He walked her to her car and began a short trek to his vehicle, which was a late model, palladium silver Mercedes-Benz C 300. It was located less than one hundred feet away. Brian continued to rub the inside of his cheek that was continually being cut by his braces.

As he neared his car, he heard his name called out from behind.

"Brian. Excuse me. Brian."

Brian turned and saw two men walking at a brisk gait to catch up to him. He stopped to allow them to catch up. The men were FBI Special Agents Pete Chrisman and Bob Malloy. Pete started to speak when they were within several feet of Brian.

"Brian, I'm Special Agent Chrisman. This is Special Agent Malloy. We're from the FBI." Pete flashed his badge as he spoke. "We'd like to ask you a few questions."

"I'm really in a hurry, fellows," Brian replied.

"This won't take long," Bob Malloy assured him.

"We understand your boss, Roger Legion, took a trip to Montana earlier this week. Do you know who he went to see?" Pete quizzed.

"I know nothing about that. You'd have to ask him," Brian shared.

"Do you handle any files in your office for an insurance company called Unibility?" Bob wondered.

"No, I don't." Brian's tone evidenced his lack of patience with the questions.

"Have you. . .," Pete started a question when Brian cut him off.

"Look, I'm done answering questions. You want to talk to me, go see my lawyer, Roger Legion," Brian flared.

"Oh, we will talk to Mr. Legion. But I only had one more question. Have you ever been to the Loma National Bank branch in Calexico, California?" Pete queried.

"Where?" Brian asked as if he didn't hear the question.

"The Loma National Bank Branch in Calexico," Bob repeated the location.

"I've never been there," Brian answered succinctly and defensively.

"Okay," Pete said. "We only ask because you fit the description of a guy who came into the bank with a Vietnamese lady and she opened a business account for a company called Copyization. So, we were just checking."

"Well, I've got to get going," Brian advised as he started walking to his car.

"We'll be in touch," Bob told him as both the agents watched him walk away.

"There's a man hiding something," Pete proclaimed.

"Just like Crazy Daisy," Bob opined.

Pete glared at Bob as if he was flabbergasted.

"I knew you were racist, but I didn't know you also hated women?" Pete said, more of a declaration than a comment.

"Of course, I do!" Bob replied. "Ask any of my many sexual conquests."

"The men or the boys," Pete retorted, trying to keep a straight face.

Pete tried to hold back a laugh, but he could not do it.

"You're a real prick," Bob told him. "You know that?"

"Word," Pete replied as they shared a quick fist bump.

CHAPTER 64

At 7:00 am, the next morning, San Diego Police Detective Margaret Byrne entered the America's Finest City Building, attempting to look as non-descript as possible. Her hair was pulled back and she wore a black Calvin Klein zip-front sheath dress with an admiral navy cashmere cardigan sweater. She carried her larger purse, which is where she kept her Sig Sauer, semi-automatic, .9 millimeter handgun.

Margaret moved directly to the Concierge Desk, removing her shield and identification from her purse as she stopped to speak.

"Excuse me," she said, getting the attention of the young man sitting at the desk as she flashed her badge. "I'd like to speak to someone about the elevator system."

The young man wore a finely tailored suit that was black cherry in color with yellow piping and his name tag read 'Reginald.'

"Again?" he asked and smiled. "You people have been here all week."

"There's always one more detail," Margaret told him.

"Oh, I know how that is. Follow me, Miss."

Reginald stood from his chair and Margaret followed him down a nearby hallway to a door that was labeled Transport

Services. He pushed a code on a keypad and a 'click' allowed him entrance.

The room was dark, except for one wall that had thirty flat screen monitors. There were three rows of ten screens. Each screen was a thirty-six-inch monitor. All the screens provided crystal clear images of 1080 pixels.

Two men, wearing the same uniform as Reginald, but also wearing headsets, sat before a large control panel that allowed them to move interior and exterior cameras, as well as control the movement of the elevators within the building. They watched loading docks for vendor activity and communicated with fire and police departments in the event of any emergency.

Margaret and Reginald walked over to the two men and Reginald tapped the older man on the shoulder.

"Candy," Reginald said, getting his attention. Candy turned to them with a smile. "This police officer has some questions."

The badge on the man's sport coat read 'Candelario.' He was in his late 50s, about 250 pounds, with a full head of salt and pepper hair and well-tanned skin.

"How can I help you?" Candy posed his inquiry as Reginald slipped out the door.

"I'd like to see that tape of the police officer being killed," Margaret requested, finding difficulty in speaking the words.

"You know I burned a copy for the officers earlier this week," Candy told her.

"If you don't mind, I'd like to see it here," Margaret shared.

"No problem. But I'm just going to warn you, it is graphic."

"I know it is," she replied with melancholy angst.

"Okay," Candy told her as he began to type. "Watch this screen over here."

He pointed to the screen that was at her eye level and approximately four feet from her face.

Margaret scrutinized the video with minute detail as she watched her partner, Detective Pete Atherton, enter the elevator with the handcuffed man posing as murdered attorney, Rike Hessler. The doors of the elevator closed and the camera was able to detect the motion of the elevator. Within seconds, the elevator stopped.

"What floor are they stopping on?" she inquired without allowing her eyes to leave the screen.

"The seventeenth," Candy answered while freezing the frame on the video.

"Okay," Margaret responded and the video again began.

A short, thin man, wearing a black, jean jacket entered the elevator. Under his jacket, he wore a hoodie, with the hood up. When the man entered the elevator, Pete Atherton moved his prisoner. Pete was now standing between his prisoner and the new elevator occupant. That occupant was obviously aware of the video camera because he kept his face turned away from it.

As soon as the door closed, the man pulled a Colt M1911 .45 caliber, semi-automatic pistol from behind his back and put it up against Pete's head. Margaret was not trained in reading lips, but she could tell that Pete was trying to reason with the man and eventually began to beg.

In an instant, the man forced Pete to remove the handcuffs from his prisoner and the Rike Hessler impersonator took possession of Pete's semi-automatic, .45 caliber, Smith & Wesson M & P 45 service weapon.

Seconds later, Pete was on his knees, in handcuffs, with the handcuffs going over the back hand railing of the elevator car. As soon as the cuffs were secure, the man claiming to be Rike Hessler, aimed Pete's gun at the back of Pete's head and pulled the trigger.

As the front of Pete's skull exploded off, blood and brain matter decorated the interior of the elevator.

The man who entered the elevator on the seventeenth floor, went over to the elevator keypad and was doing something off-view of the monitoring camera. The video showed the elevator coming to a jarring stop.

"What's he doing there?" Margaret quizzed with her eyes remaining locked on the video.

"We think that he's clearing the memory on the elevator and then sending it directly back to the twenty-fourth floor," Candy relayed.

"How many people here know how to do that?" she wondered.

Candy thought about it for a moment.

"Six, including me."

"I want to get those names," Margaret requested.

"Okay, but we gave them to another policeman right after the incident."

"If you don't mind, I'd like to get my own copy. Let's finish the video."

Candy unfroze the video. It showed the two men exiting on the ninth floor, the doors closing, and a non-stop return trip began to the twenty-fourth floor.

"You all set?" Candy asked Margaret.

"I want to see it again," Margaret requested in a tone that indicated deep thought.

Candy again cued up the video and it began. As the video reached the point where the new elevator occupant put his gun to Pete Atherton's head, Margaret spoke up.

"Stop!" Candy heeded her command. "Can you back it up a few frames?"

Candy did as requested.

"Let's see it frame by frame," Margaret directed.

Candy began to slowly advance the video, when Margaret spoke up again.

"Stop!"

In the video frame, the passenger's arm was fully extended, while pointing the gun at Pete's head. It was then that Margaret uttered a revelation.

"That coat doesn't fit him. Can you enhance the image?"

Candy began and enhanced the picture by 400 percent. When the man lifted his arm, it was evident that the coat pulled oddly under his arm.

"I want to see the buttonhole areas on this guy's jean jacket," she told him while pointing to the gunman."

Candy obliged and panned the picture in the area she desired.

"Stop," Margaret told him as she examined what she saw. On one of the buttonholes was a small piece of paper looped through the hole. The color of the paper matched the coat. Margaret knew that this type of paper was normally attached to an article of clothing after cleaning.

"Can I see a list of all the vendors who were in the building that day?"

"No you can't," came a voice from behind her.

She turned and saw Detective Ray Abernathy, a seasoned San Diego policeman, who was in charge of the Pete Atherton murder investigation. He was a twenty-seven year veteran of the force and looked more like a grandfather than a policeman.

"Ray, let me just look at it," Margaret pleaded. "I've got a hunch."

"Margaret, you're supposed to be on administrative leave. Last time I checked, they don't have any hotel rooms in this building."

"Let me just follow up on something," her pleading continued.

"If it's about the dry cleaning, we have men on it right now," Ray told her.

"And?"

"And what?" Ray flared. "They're pounding the pavement. As soon as we get something, we'll act on it. And, as I recall, I don't report to you."

"Ray. I'm begging you. Let me help," Margaret's plea was more of a demand.

"NO! Margaret, he knows what you look like. If he sees you, he won't come within a mile of this place. I've got a team of people in the lobby and throughout the building. I can have a SWAT team on the twenty-fourth floor within five minutes."

"How do you plan on doing that?" she questioned in disbelief.

"They're on standby. We're going to insert them through the roof." Ray stared at Margaret for a moment. "Now, are you going to leave, or do I have to call the Captain and have him ask you to leave?"

Margaret turned to Candy.

"Thanks, Candy."

"You're welcome," he replied.

Ray walked Margaret out of the building.

"Don't come back, Margaret. It's too dangerous."

"You know, Ray, Pete Atherton had little kids. One day, those kids are going to ask somebody 'How did my dad die?' And those kids are going to be told, 'His partner killed him.' That's why I'm here."

Ray looked at her and didn't utter a word. He knew she was in pain and was right. Margaret walked to her car, got in, and drove away. Her efforts to catch a killer had only just begun.

CHAPTER 65

Judge Harrison Ogilvie gazed at his visage in his bathroom mirror and looked for any lines or crow's feet around his eyes. He straightened his suspenders and his bowtie. He wore a blue and white striped shirt and navy blue slacks.

He took a rattail comb from one of the bathroom drawers and pulled it through his white hair, wanting to make sure every hair was perfectly in place. When he was done, he looked at the comb for a moment and remembered some of the places that this comb had visited. He had washed the pointy handle of it on more occasions than he cared to remember.

As he stared at the comb, he thought about US Assistant Attorney General Daisy Zacaro. He thought that she would enjoy being sodomized by the comb by some of her friends, who were probably lesbians. What Judge Ogilvie preferred would be to puncture her eyes with it for daring to place him in a stressful situation. He planned on giving her a tongue-lashing, so that she knew to avoid him in the future.

The Judge checked his pocket for the famous tape of Roger Legion disclosing all the secrets of Vici Resolutions. He planned to go directly to the Attorney General's Office to hand deliver the tape.

He removed his black, button cardigan from the hall closet and set the perimeter alarm for his condominium. He moved directly to the elevator for a brisk ride to the parking garage.

The Judge dashed to his Lincoln Continental and accelerated from his parking space to the nearest exit. The Vivro Towers required an access card to enter and exit the parking facility.

He swiped the card and a gate raised to allow him passage onto Market Street.

As he accelerated to move into traffic, a gargantuan explosion erupted from underneath the car. The blast was so enormous that it snapped the car in two at the driver's seat. Each portion of the car flipped onto its roof. The accompanying fireball was so monstrous, it rose seven stories in the air.

The murder of Judge Harrison Ogilvie was about to become front page news. The FBI would be called in to investigate the bomb used to kill the Judge. And Daisy Zacaro wanted to make sure that the San Diego Police Department had Roger Legion in their sights.

CHAPTER 66

The temperature in Santa Isabella, located in the State of Chihuahua, Mexico at 1:00 pm was ninety-six degrees. Glenn Edgarian spent the last twenty-four hours sitting in a dank, roach-infested cell waiting for a delivery from Roger Legion of fifteen thousand dollars. This was the amount demanded by local Police Chief Luz for Glenn's release.

Glenn was unaware of the full extent of his squalor-laden surroundings because his abductors removed his contact lenses. Time was of the essence because Chief Luz advised Glenn that he had signed a confession claiming to be a drug smuggler and had been sentenced to twenty-two years in federal prison. He was now awaiting a prison transport bus.

The heat and humidity caused the stench of feces and urine to be amplified. Glenn had not had anything to drink since he took a sip of his Americano coffee in the Starbucks parking lot where he was abducted. His shirt was soaking wet and every time he closed his eyes, in an attempt to sleep, he felt some kind of bug crawling up his leg or arm.

Chief Luz was in his office, sitting at his desk, enjoying a large, egg and bean burrito that he brought from home with a large bottle of Coca-Cola. Three other deputies, all men, were working on various paperwork and preparing assignments for the next week's activities.

The reception area of the police station was small with a counter that divided the room in half. Behind it were three desks, stacked with papers and computers that were at least a decade old. The walls were crème colored and showing every moment of their age.

A man entered from the sun-drenched street and casually surveyed the premises. He wore a chocolate, Stetson Rambler hat with a four-inch brim. He also wore a black sport coat, a yellow and blue checkered button-front shirt, and jeans. On his feet were handmade Lucchese cowboy boots made of hornback caiman, a type of crocodile skin. His sunglasses reflected like mirrors and a toothpick bobbed up and down from his mouth as if it was the man's pulse.

He carried a briefcase and moved in a somewhat defined manner. He was thin and lanky, clean-shaven, six feet tall and no more than 160 pounds. He removed his sunglasses from his face down to the counter.

"*Hola* (Hello)," he called out to get the attention of one of deputies.

"*¿Puedo ayudarle?* (Can I help you?)" the deputy asked.

"I'm here to see Chief Luz. I'm a lawyer for one of your prisoners."

The deputy called to the Chief in Spanish and he emerged from his office, wiping his mouth with the back of his hand and forearm.

"How can I help you?" the Chief asked.

"I'm here for Glenn Edgarian. I'm his lawyer."

"Did you bring something with you?" the Chief again inquired.

"I did. But I need to see my client first. You know, proof of life," the man replied without stopping the movement of his toothpick.

The Chief then pointed to a door in the corner of the room.

"Through that door is the cells. He's down at the end."

"Why don't you go get him?" the man told him.

"Give me what you brought and I'll go get him."

"I can't do that."

The Chief and the man looked at each other as if locked in a stalemate. The Chief then snapped his fingers to get the attention of a deputy sitting at a desk between him and the door.

"*Abre la puerta!* (Open the door!)" he commanded.

The deputy followed his instruction and the Chief looked back at the man.

"Call to him. He can hear you," the Chief advised.

"GLENN!" the man shouted.

"YEAH," Glenn shouted back.

"ROGER LEGION SAYS 'HELLO.' HANG TIGHT. WE'RE GOING TO BE OUT OF HERE SHORTLY."

The Chief stared at the man.

"You happy now? And what's your name?" the Chief asked.

"Joe."

The blood drained from the Chief's face and a look of concern covered it.

"I heard stories," the Chief told him, "about a guy named Joe the Lawyer. They say he's a cleaner. High end. They say if you get in a gunfight with him, you better kill him with your first bullet, because you won't get a second."

241

The Chief's 'cleaner' comment indicated that Joe the Lawyer was a high-paid assassin.

"He sounds kind of interesting," Joe answered with his eyes moving methodically from the Chief to the various deputies.

Inside his cell, Glenn sat in a weakened state with his head resting in his hands with perspiration dripping off his chin and nose, forming a small puddle on the floor.

Suddenly, the barking of dogs outside was drowned out by the eruption of a gun battle in the reception area of the police station. Glenn rose to his feet, walking over to the bars of the door to the cell to get a glimpse of what was going on. One extraordinary sounding weapon was blaring in what seemed to sound like mechanical repetition until there was sudden silence. It was not like a machine gun, but more like a finely tuned engine. Within ten seconds, it was over.

Glenn had no idea what had happened and his lack of accurate vision only served to heighten his concern for the man who came to have him released.

"HEY!" Glenn called out. "ANYBODY OUT THERE?"

In a flash, Joe appeared moving quickly with a large keyring, searching for the cell master key. He tried two or three keys and was finally able to open the cell.

"Let's go," Joe told him and they raced directly out of the building. Waiting outside was a candy-apple red, 1975 Cadillac El Dorado convertible. Joe and Glenn got in and took off.

What Glenn could not see as they exited was that Joe efficiently killed the three deputies and the Chief. The stories that the chief had heard about Joe the Lawyer were true. None of the dead men fired a second shot.

CHAPTER 67

As dusk turned into night, Brian Stensler pulled into the underground parking garage of the Skyline Plaza Apartments, located in the City Heights section of San Diego. This area consisted of mostly older homes and had a slightly higher crime rate than other areas of San Diego. This apartment complex was nearly fifty years old.

Legion attorney, Ned Chandler, had lived in this apartment house for the past three years. He would always talk about moving, but his actions never went beyond the talking stage.

Brian locked his Mercedes C 300 and took a quick elevator ride to the third floor, Apartment 304. He knocked and Ned answered immediately.

"Hey, come on in. You want something to drink?"

"No. I'm good," Brian replied.

"Hey, what did you think about your buddy, Ogilvie?" Ned inquired. "He must have pissed off somebody real good."

Ned was referencing the Judge, whose car exploded that morning.

"Couldn't have happened to a nicer guy," Brian shared.

Brian entered the sparsely furnished, living room and there, sitting on the couch, was Michael Eiffert. Michael and Brian were still wearing their suits from earlier in the day. Ned was dressed casually in a t-shirt and jeans.

"How do, Kimosabe? How are your braces?" Mike asked.

"I can't wait to get them off. So, what's the big rush that you need me down here?" Brian asked.

"We need to talk about the adventure," Mike shared.

"I don't want to talk about it," Brian replied. "I want to forget about it."

"Well," Mike began, "the money's not going anyplace. The Feds put a hold on it and they're going to snag anybody who tries to touch it."

"So, it was all for nothing?" Brian asked.

"Mike's got a way that we can still salvage something from it."

"What do you suggest, O great, Montana, crime Svengali?" Brian's voice dripped with sarcasm.

"I need you guys to fall on your sword. Admit what you did. Tell Legion there was no ill intent. Just a simple *mea culpa*," Mike suggested.

"A simple *mea culpa*? Are you out of your goddamned mind?" Brian flared. "What do you think Roger Legion would do to us once he found out? There's a Memorial Plaque in the reception area of lawyers who have tried to get something over on him in the past. Five years ago, you were probably a heartbeat away from being one of them."

"I can smooth it over," Mike retorted. "You won't lose your jobs."

"Yeah?" Brian flared. "Well, the FBI wanted to talk to me in the parking lot of North County Courthouse yesterday. They were asking me about Unibility files and that I fit the description of a guy who accompanied a Vietnamese lady to the Loma National Bank in Calexico."

"They were just rousting you," Mike declared. "They got nothing. They talked to three other guys from the firm yesterday and gave them all the same speech. You do what I tell you and everything will be fine."

"Do you agree with this shit?" Brian asked Ned. Ned shrugged his shoulders.

"Mike said he may be able to get us a little cash if we go along," Ned conveyed.

"Ned, we have committed a federal crime. Every time we did it is another count. The federal government is not going to let us walk on this."

"They'll never know," Mike interjected. "Legion will want to keep it quiet. He'll work a deal. Just tell him the truth."

"The truth?" Brian announced as he glared at Mike. "Oh, the truth. You mean the truth where *you* originally came up with the idea. *You* sold it to us. *You* showed us how to set up the phony copy company, Copyization. *You* told us how to set up the bank account. *You* said to use Ned's girlfriend's aunt as one of the signatories on the account. *You* told us to set it up out in Calexico. And *you* were going to move the money for us. Is that the truth you want me to tell?"

"You want my help or not?" Mike quizzed. "I'm handing you a life preserver and you want to drown."

"If I drown, I'm not going to drown alone," Brian asserted.

"Think about it," Mike announced and walked directly out of the apartment.

"We have to come up with an end game for this, because I don't trust him," Brian disclosed. "If we do it his way, we are going to either lose our law licenses or wind up on that Memorial Plaque. I don't like either of those options."

"Let's talk about it tomorrow," Ned told him.

Brian left Ned's apartment for a quick elevator ride to the underground garage. He clicked the fob key to unlock the car doors.

Once inside the car, he grabbed his seat belt to pull it across and suddenly, without warning, the driver's window was shattered by four .45 caliber, hallow point bullets, fired in rapid succession. All four bullets struck Brian in the head, blowing large chunks of his skull and brain matter onto the passenger seat and window.

One of the bullets struck his upper jaw and decimated most of his top teeth. They were blasted out of his skull. The metal wires of his braces were still connected to one of his back teeth and hung down on the right side of his skull. He finally received one of the things he wanted: his braces removed.

Brian would also receive one of the things he did not want. A place on the Memorial Plaque at Legion & Associates.

CHAPTER 68

After a day of death in San Diego and Santa Isabella, Mexico, Special Agent Brenda Tomaras returned home shortly after 8:00 pm. A blanket of darkness covered her split-level ranch home. She pulled into her garage and decided to check the mail before entering. The residential mailboxes were grouped into sets of twelve and Brenda's was located in front of a home that was two houses down.

She retrieved the mail and glanced through it quickly to see if anything interesting arrived. One of the letters caught her attention. It was a plain, white envelope that was addressed, in block letters, to 'Brenda 'Sparkplug' Tomaras.' The postmark was from Miami, Florida. No one outside of the FBI was aware of that nickname, except for her husband and George Lorin, the mastermind of the armored truck heist, in which the money from the Mondo Run was seized and twelve men were killed.

Brenda stood inside her lighted garage and opened the letter. It contained a single piece of white paper and stated the following:

If you want to catch George Lorin, go to San Diego and look in the trunk of a Cadillac owned by an attorney named

Roger Legion. Under the spare tire, you will find a big piece of the puzzle.

Brenda was perplexed at the letter's contents. She immediately knew that it was George Lorin baiting her.

She entered her home and spoke briefly to her husband and daughter, then moved directly to the family office to review some information on the internet.

Brenda determined that Roger Legion was an attorney in San Diego and she also read the recent news article about a police detective being killed after arresting a suspect in Legion's office. She then picked up the phone and called an old friend from the FBI Academy, who was assigned to the San Diego office. It was Bob Malloy, the same special agent who had been surveilling Roger Legion and assisting US Assistant Attorney General Daisy Zacaro in her investigation of Legion.

Brenda shared with Bob the details surrounding the Mondo Run heist and her interaction with George Lorin that put her in a coma for four days. She was reluctant to disclose the note that she received to the head of the task force investigating the matter. She knew that the author of the note wanted her to be there when the trunk was searched.

"Do you think he would let us voluntarily search it or do we need a warrant?" Brenda inquired.

"This guy's a lawyer, so he's probably going to give us a tough time," Bob replied. "I think he's hiding something. But a lot of people that I spoke to think he is a great guy. So, we can ask. The most he can say is 'No.' And we have the car under surveillance with a tracker on it."

"Now, tell me why you've got eyes on this guy," Brenda wondered.

Bob told her that a certain United States Assistant Attorney General, whom he referred to as Crazy Daisy, had a vendetta against Legion. He said the reasons were unknown to him. The case that Daisy was working up against Legion involved wire and mail fraud. He deduced that it must also involve several of Legion's attorneys.

He knew of no connection to Sandpoint, Idaho by Legion, but he told her that Legion did travel to Great Falls, Montana the week before. Bob had no information on why Legion went or who he saw.

"I'm going to come to San Diego tomorrow," Brenda disclosed. "I've got a sister who lives in Poway, over there. I'm going to tell the bosses in Coeur d'Alene and Salt Lake City that I'm taking vacation. I want to go with you to talk with Mr. Legion. And Bob, don't share this intel with your bosses."

"Roger that," he confirmed.

By early afternoon of the next day, Brenda was on a plane headed to San Diego. She was glad that Bob would be there to back her up, just in case it was a trap.

CHAPTER 69

Roger Legion slowly lowered his landline telephone receiver to its cradle and let out a sigh under his breath. He swiveled the seat of his chair for a view of the ocean and gazed at the splendor of the horizon. He was just informed that one of his attorneys, Brian Stensler, was found murdered in a parking garage in the City Heights section of San Diego.

Roger had been through this before and he was never able to get over the pain he felt for every attorney he lost. Like a child that dies before his time, it brought agony and misery to Legion. His goal had always been to turn men into feared warriors who would dispense justice, but he wanted none of them to pay this price. In another time and another place, he would probably shed a tear, but not here and not now.

His thoughts were interrupted by a rap on his door. Mike Eiffert knocked as he marched in at a quick gait. They looked at each other for a moment and Roger wondered if Mike had heard the news.

"I know who sent out the phony bills?" Mike declared with urgency.

"Who?" Roger exclaimed, matching his urgency.

"Brian Stensler and Ned Chandler," Mike shared. "We were talking yesterday and Ned asked me to come over to his place last night."

"So, you didn't hear?" Legion asked.

"Hear what?" Mike wondered.

"They found Brian Stensler in a parking garage with most of his head blown off."

"Where?" Mike quizzed in disbelief.

"City Heights."

Mike stood there with his mouth partially open.

"That's where Ned lives," Mike disclosed apologetically.

"Are you sure those are the guys?" Legion asked, requesting certainty.

"Yes."

Legion picked up his landline phone and pressed two numbers.

"Nina, if Ned Chandler comes in, call me, but don't let him know that I'm looking for him." As he hung up the phone, his cell phone, which sat on the desk, began to vibrate. "I want to discuss this later," he told Mike. "I've already spoken to the cops. Tell Nina if any police come in here, she should direct them to me."

Mike nodded affirmatively and scurried out the door. Legion answered his cell phone.

"Roger Legion."

"Roger, it's Kez. I'm calling to see if it's done."

Kez was Keswick Thompkins, the General Counsel for a company called Zunkunft. Zunkunft retained Roger Legion to pay off a blackmailer who claimed to have pornographic images of their CEO with children. Roger determined that the one photograph that he was provided had been manipulated, but the company still wanted the money paid.

The police tried to arrest the blackmailer at Legion's office and the blackmailer killed one of the police officers.

"Not yet," Legion responded. "I don't call him, he calls me."

"Well," Kez began, "I just got some news that changes the landscape. Our IPO (initial public offering) is not going forward. I say pull the plug on the payment."

"All right," Roger told him with a tone of frustration. "But other than that one picture, I don't know what he's got. If this whole thing was never true, then why did your company consider paying the guy in the first place?"

"I told you there were practical and economic reasons associated with it," Kez exclaimed.

"I can't keep it quiet. The guy killed a cop."

"Work your magic. That's what I pay you for."

With that, the call abruptly ended. It was then that he saw Nina standing in his doorway holding her cellphone.

"He's on the phone," she uttered with dread.

Legion waved her in and took the phone from her hand.

"This is Roger Legion."

"Mr. Legion, I will be short and to the point. I wish to conclude our business activities. I shall come into your office within the next seventy-two hours at sometime between 8:00 am and 6:30 pm. Please be sure that you are available. As soon as I confirm the transfer, I will sign whatever document you desire. The name to place on the document is Otto Stern. Now, do you understand how we are going to proceed?"

"Yes," he answered with deadpan certainty.

"One final thing: If I detect any police presence in or around your building, I will be left with no choice, but to not move forward with our transaction and blame you for its failure. The penalty will be quite substantial. *Auf Wiedersehen* (Goodbye.)"

With that the call ended. Legion handed the phone back to Nina.

"Thank you, Nina."

She simply smiled and returned to her desk.

When Roger thought back on all of his days as a lawyer, this was one of his worst. A Legion lawyer had been struck down in his prime. Roger did not care about what damage he may have caused the firm. All he could think about was the greatness that was wasted.

As for this new threat from the now-revealed Otto Stern, Legion had three days or less to come up with a plan to stop him. The clock was running.

Legion's cell phone again began to vibrate. He picked it up and looked at the Caller ID. It was from San Diego Police Detective Margaret Byrne. He sent the call to voicemail. The rest of the day would be non-eventful.

CHAPTER 70

The next morning, US Assistant Attorney General Daisy Zacaro took a long sip of her dark roast coffee, served black, and as hot as could be tolerated. She had just completed a conference call with a San Diego Police Captain, in charge of the Homicide Division, to discuss the formation of a Joint Task force to investigate the murder of Judge Harrison Ogilvie. Also on the call was a bomb technician supervisor to provide initial information on the bomb used to blow up and kill Judge Ogilvie. Her frustration was evident.

Daisy's only goal was to point them in the direction of Roger Legion. But because Legion had been under surveillance, the San Diego Police were reluctant to elevate him to a person of interest. They wanted more information and Daisy promised it.

When she was asked about what Federal crimes she was investigating that involved a State Superior Court Justice, she danced around the question, only to say that it involved wire and mail fraud.

The bomb technician supervisor indicated that the bomb used to kill Judge Ogilvie appeared to be a Confetti bomb. It is highly technical and considered a cocktail of various plastic explosives, coupled with dynamite. Prior to this incident, the FBI knew of its use in a failed armored truck robbery in Wyoming and the recent armored truck robbery involving the Mondo Run outside of Sandpoint, Idaho. The device was considered highly technical and custom-built.

As she considered her next move, she glanced at the newspaper for that day. On the second page of the LOCAL section, there was an article about a local attorney found murdered in the parking garage of an apartment complex in City Heights. The name, Brian Stensler, sounded familiar and she began a quick review of the daily reports provided by Special Agents Chrisman and Malloy.

The Special Agents had spoken to Brian Stensler the day before he died. The newspaper article mentioned that he was an attorney, but did not mention that he worked at Legion & Associates.

Daisy knew that Legion's influence was able to keep his name out of the paper. She was sure that the death of this attorney had something to do with her case involving fraudulent billing and Unibility Insurance.

She turned in her chair as quickly as it could move and dialed Special Agent Peter Chrisman. The call went to voicemail.

"Where are you?" she fumed. "Call me. Now."

The Special Agents were in the elevator of the America's Finest City Building, with no telephone reception, accompanying Brenda Tomaras to the office of Legion & Associates.

"When we get there, you do the talking," Pete told Brenda.

"All right," she replied just as the elevator car reached the twenty-fourth floor. The three of them exited the car and Brenda walked directly to the receptionist, Nina, without noticing the opulence of the lobby.

"Hi, we're here to see Roger Legion. I'm Special Agent Brenda Tomaras. This is Special Agent Bob Malloy and Special Agent Pete Chrisman. We're all from the FBI."

Bob wore a charcoal, gray suit and Pete wore a gray pinstripe suit. Brenda wore an industrial blue, solid-knit blazer with matching pants and a white, turtleneck sweater under the blazer.

"Do you have an appointment?" Nina wondered.

"I'm sorry. No, we don't."

"Okay, hold one second," Nina advised and called Legion through the intercom system.

Back in his office, Roger was reviewing the contract he drafted that was going to be between Zunkunft and Otto Stern, the man attempting to blackmail the company. This day he wore a solid, black suit with a silk tie that had a black and red diamond pattern.

"Yes," Roger answered to Nina's call.

"There are three Special Agents here from the FBI to see you."

"Send them to the conference room and I'll be right there."

"All the conference rooms are being used right now."

"Send them back to my office."

Nina then turned her attention back to Brenda.

"Go down this hallway all the way. The last office on the left."

Brenda thanked her and they moved at a quick pace to Legion's office. As soon as he saw them in the doorway, he rose to invite them in.

"Come on in," Roger said as he waved them in.

Brenda walked directly up to him and offered him a firm handshake as she spoke.

"Hello, Mr. Legion. I'm Special Agent Brenda Tomaras from the Coeur d'Alene office of the FBI. This is Special Agent

Bob Malloy and Special Agent Pete Chrisman of out San Diego office."

"I'm familiar with these gentlemen," Legion shared. "They enjoy watching me."

The comment brought a smile to Bob Malloy's face.

"Mr. Legion," Brenda began, "I'm investigating an armored truck robbery that took place on the Friday before Labor Day, just outside of Sandpoint, Idaho. There were twelve people killed that day, including two Idaho state troopers. We believe that one man killed all of the people that day. He killed not only law enforcement, but the armored truck crew and his confederates that assisted him with the robbery."

"I don't wish to be flippant," Legion commented, "but what does this have to do with me?"

"Do you know a man named George Lorin?" Brenda asked.

Roger shook his head and answered, "No."

"I had the unfortunate experience of interacting with Mr. Lorin. I ended up with a black eye, cracked rib, and I was in a coma for four days."

Legion could only stare in disbelief.

"Do you have a picture of this guy?" Legion asked.

"No. But he sent me a letter," Brenda explained as she pulled out a copy of the letter from her purse and showed it to Legion, "saying that I should come to San Diego and look in the trunk of your car to catch this guy."

Roger studied the letter and handed it back to her.

"Well, let's go look," he said.

The four of them exited Legion's office on their way to the parking garage. All of them, including Legion, had a heightened curiosity in regard to what they were about to find.

CHAPTER 71

Candelario or Candy sat at his viewing station inside the Transport Services office making sure that everything that moved within the America's Finest City Building went smoothly. He had just called an ambulance for an elderly woman who appeared to collapse after entering an elevator on the seventh floor. The security people determined that she was suffering from low blood sugar, but she was being sent to the hospital as a precaution.

Candy always kept his cell phone out on his desktop and preferred talking to friends via text messages, so that his business would not be broadcast to unwanted ears. When his phone did ring, it was rather unusual.

As he took a sip from a bottle of water, his phone went off, playing the Blondie song, *Call Me*. He looked at the Caller ID, but did not recognize the number. Candy decided to answer it.

"Hello," he answered in a somewhat restrained voice.

"Candy, this is Detective Margaret Byrne of the San Diego Police Department. We met earlier this week. You showed me a video tape."

"Oh yeah, hi. How are you doing?"

"I'm fine," Margaret told him. "I just had a few more questions that maybe you could help me answer."

"Sure. Go ahead," Candy answered as he continued to view the video monitors.

"Is there a mobile dry cleaning service or clothes washing service that comes to the building?"

Margaret was following up on her hunch that the man with Otto Stern in the elevator when Margaret's partner, Pete Atherton, was murdered wore a jean jacket that did not fit and it also had a dry cleaning tag on it.

"Bay Valet Detail," Candy responded immediately.

"Detail?" Margaret wondered.

"Yeah, they wash your car and your clothes."

"Were they in the building the day the policeman was killed?" Margaret quizzed.

"They were," Candy said. "But they had no deliveries on any floor higher than the twelfth."

"When are they scheduled to be there again?"

"Hold on a sec," Candy hesitated. "I don't see them on the schedule for any time in the near future. Sometimes they just show up last minute and we confirm it with the tenant."

Margaret paused to think for a moment.

"I know you can watch the interior of the elevator. Can you also control it?" she quizzed.

"Absolutely," Candy replied. "I can stop any elevator between floors and I can open and close any of the doors, even if the car isn't there."

"It just opens to the elevator shaft?" Margaret queried.

"Yeah," Candy told her, "but there's a special alarm that goes off to put people on notice that there's no car there, just in case they're too stupid to realize it."

"Candy, thanks for your help. Would it be okay if I call you again if I have any questions?"

"Sure. No problem," he shared. "Whatever you need. And I know that it's nobody's business that we talked."

"Thank you, Candy."

Margaret was in her car, parked just three blocks from the America's Finest City Building when the phone call ended. The person she now wanted to speak with was Roger Legion.

CHAPTER 72

Special Agents Bob Malloy, Pete Chrisman, and Brenda Tomaras, along with Roger Legion, emerged from the elevator into the parking garage of the building. Legion's late-model, black Cadillac CTS was parked less than one hundred feet from the bank of elevators.

Legion pointed to his car, took out his key fob, and handed it to Brenda.

"Gentlemen," she said, addressing the other two Special Agents, "do you have gloves?"

The three FBI personnel put on blue latex gloves and Brenda popped open the trunk using the fob. The interior of the trunk was pristine, there was nothing inside, but a carpeted trunk liner.

Bob Malloy and Pete Chrisman began the task of removing the trunk liner, while Brenda had a few more questions for Legion.

"Does anyone else drive this car?"

"No," Legion responded.

"Does anyone else have access to it?"

"No."

"Do you park it in a garage at night?"

"Yes."

"Has it been anyplace out of the ordinary lately?" Brenda wondered.

"You should ask your two friends, here. They've been following me and I assume they have a tracker, so they know where it's been."

As Legion finished his sentence, Pete Chrisman was removing a wingnut from the top of the spare tire compartment. The car had a full-size spare tire and the area where it was kept was recessed into the body of the vehicle.

Pete pulled the spare tire out of the trunk and set it down against the bumper. All four of the individuals leaned in to see what was within the tire well. There they saw what appeared to be a steel tile. It was twelve by twelve inches and one and one-half inches thick. It also had four small, circular metal legs.

Brenda immediately sprang into reaction mode.

"Call the Bomb Squad! Let's get out of here," she said as she hurried the other three men away from the car. "Call local law enforcement. Get them to clear the area."

"What is it?" Bob Malloy wondered.

"It's a car bomb. It's called a Confetti. It got that name because that's what it turns a car into. It's a mix of various plastic explosives, coupled with dynamite. It was used to stop the armored truck in my Sandpoint case."

Pete Chrisman walked back to the car and again looked into the tire well. He reached into it to grab something. Bob Malloy was on the phone with the San Diego Metro Arson Strike Team or MAST. MAST is responsible for the removal of any suspected explosive devices.

"Pete," Brenda called out to him, "this guy would like nothing more than to kill three FBI agents and a lawyer."

"Not if he wants us to find something," Pete replied.

Pete walked back to the group, now standing by the elevators, and he handed Brenda several strips of paper that were located in the tire well.

On the strips of paper was the logo from the Gemstone National Bank in Sandpoint, Idaho and a date stamp for the Friday before Labor Day, the date of the Mondo Run robbery.

"These are money bands from the robbery in Sandpoint." She then turned to Legion. "Do you know anything about these items?"

"I've never seen them before," Legion announced with certainty.

Just then, Pete Chrisman's cell phone rang and his face turned disgusted as he viewed the Caller ID.

"Yeah," he answered.

"WHERE HAVE YOU BEEN!?" Daisy exploded when she heard his voice. "I have been trying to call you and you don't return my calls."

"We've been busy," Pete responded with no-nonsense flair.

"Doing what? Having gay sex? Where are you? And don't lie to me or I'll have you terminated from the FBI before the end of the day."

"We're in the parking garage of the America's Finest City Building. We're with Roger Legion and we're looking in the trunk of his car."

"Do you have a warrant?" she quizzed.

"No, he gave permission," Pete told her.

"Listen to me," Daisy fumed. "He's using you, you idiot! Legion would never let you look in his trunk. He wants you to find whatever you're gonna find!"

"I don't think so, Daisy," Pete retorted.

"I want you and your girlfriend and anybody you have with you from the FBI to come to my office right now! You hear me!" Daisy seethed with rage.

"Yeah," Pete calmly replied.

"Put Legion on the phone," she demanded.

Pete handed his cell phone to Roger Legion.

"Daisy Zacaro," Pete informed Roger.

"Hello," Roger answered.

"I see in the paper that you murdered another one of your attorneys." Daisy's speech was cold and detached. "Was he the guy stealing from Unibility? I know you like to hand out justice swiftly over there."

"I have no idea what you're talking about," Roger responded.

"You will soon. The end is in sight." Daisy then slammed the telephone receiver down.

Legion handed the cell phone back to Pete Chrisman.

"I should get back to my office," Legion told Brenda.

"Okay," she replied.

Legion entered an elevator for a direct, non-stop ride to the twenty-fourth floor. Roger would be introspective for the next few hours going over the events of the recent past.

CHAPTER 73

Ninety minutes after speaking with US Assistant Attorney General Daisy Zacaro, Special Agents Chrisman, Malloy, and Tomaras entered her office. They stood in front of her desk as Daisy eyeballed them from her chair. She suddenly stood to address them.

"Who's your little girlfriend here?" she asked Malloy and Chrisman.

"Special Agent Brenda Tomaras from the Coeur d'Alene office," Pete Chrisman responded.

"What is Special Agent Brenda Tomaras doing in America's Finest City?" Daisy inquired.

"May I answer that?" Brenda interjected.

"No, you may not," Daisy replied angrily.

"She's here investigating an armored truck robbery that took place outside of Sandpoint, Idaho on the Friday before Labor Day," Pete told her.

"The Mondo Run?" Daisy inquired.

"Yes," Brenda said. "I received a letter," Brenda told her as she removed the note from her purse to show Daisy, "that said if I wanted to catch the guy responsible for the Mondo Run robbery, I should come to San Diego and look in the trunk of Roger Legion's car."

"So, you asked and he said, yes?"

"I think he was as curious as we were," Brenda shared.

"What did you find?" Daisy's question was more in the form of a demand.

"A bomb. Referred to as a Confetti and money bands from the Mondo Run robbery," Brenda told her.

"Did you arrest him?" She posed the question to all three agents.

"I believe he was being set-up by the real perpetrator," Brenda declared.

"What if I was to tell you," Daisy claimed, "that I was set to have a meeting earlier this week with a California Superior Court judge, who was going to bring me an audio tape of Roger Legion talking about his involvement in a judicial corruption scandal? When the Judge pulled out of his parking garage that morning, his car exploded. And you know what type of bomb was used? A Confetti."

The agents had no response to Daisy's disclosure.

"Roger Legion doesn't get set-up, he sets people up," Daisy continued. "On the same day that Judge was murdered, one of Legion's attorneys was murdered in an underground parking lot. That attorney was part of another investigation I have involving mail and wire fraud at the Legion law firm. Do you still think he's being set-up, Brenda?"

"I met the guy who was the mastermind of the Mondo Run robbery," Brenda stated. "I know it wasn't Legion."

"The problem is, that asshole has the three of you twisted around his finger. Agent Chrisman," Daisy declared.

"Yes, ma'am," he responded.

"Now, I want you to go back to your office and re-evaluate the evidence you have in this case. I want you to determine if there is enough probable cause to arrest Roger Legion for the armored truck heist, the murder of Judge Ogilvie, or jaywalking. And we both know how much probable cause we need, right?"

Daisy stopped her speech to blow on her fingers to motion that next to no probable cause was needed to get a warrant.

"Then, I want you to prepare an arrest warrant. I want *you* to do it, not a flunky. You call me when it's ready and I'll tell you where to send it for a signature. When you get it back, you and I and your dark-colored girlfriend," she said referring to Agent Malloy, "are going to see Roger Legion and arrest him. Are we on the same page here?" She paused for a moment. "Anything less, and I would have to assume you were being derelict in your duty as a Federal officer."

Special Agent Bob Malloy shook his head with a minor smile.

"Is something funny, Special Agent?" Daisy asked referring to Malloy. "I thought maybe you were just thinking about when you were a kid, sitting around the shack, remembering the stink of chitlins and collard greens, while you waited for the welfare check on the first of the month. Because you were owed? Right?"

Silence shrouded the room.

"You really are Crazy Daisy," Malloy voiced his opinion with seething anger.

"Bob, let it go," Pete cut Bob off before anything was said that he would regret.

"Now, I know how to get a rise out of you. Treat you like the piece of shit you are. You want to take a swing at me?" Daisy welcomed her dare.

"I'm sure I would hit you so hard that I would break my hand on your face," Malloy assured her.

"Do it," she dared him again. "Do it. And I'll have you on the next boat back to Africa."

"Let's go," Pete spoke up to cut the tension.

"Brenda," Daisy interjected. "Do your bosses know that you're here?"

"No. They think I'm visiting my sister in Poway," she responded.

"Don't you think you should tell them, based on what you found?"

"Yes, ma'am."

"All right, then. Get out!" Daisy flared.

As usual, nothing was said among the agents until the elevators had closed. Pete Chrisman looked at Brenda.

"Welcome to paradise," he conveyed.

Brenda believed it was more like an island of madness. She kept thinking that George Lorin is right in front of her, but there is something that she is missing.

CHAPTER 74

As soon as Roger Legion stepped off the elevator and onto the twenty-fourth floor, the voice of Nina, the receptionist, got his attention.

"Ned Chandler is on line seven," she said. "He's been on hold for quite a while."

Ned Chandler and Brian Stensler formulated the plot to steal money from Unibility Insurance using fraudulent billing invoices from a copy service they created. The mastermind behind the plot was Michael Eiffert.

"Tell him I'll be right with him," Legion told her and darted directly to his office. He took his seat at his desk and pushed the line seven button on his phone.

"Hello, Ned," Roger answered with his voice meted and calm like a poker player keeping a straight face.

"Roger, you've got to help me. I think I'm going to be next."

"Next for what?" Roger quizzed.

"A one-way trip to the morgue," Ned responded with a rushed voice.

As Ned finished his sentence, Legion began to hear a crackling or scratching sound on the phone line. This indicated that the FBI was listening in on the call.

"Tell me what the problem is, Ned," Legion asked continuing to stay calm.

"Brian Stensler and I were sending phony bills to Unibility Insurance for a company called Copyization. The FBI is on to it, because they froze the money and some FBI guys talked to Brian about it. He freaked out and said if he was going down, he was going to take everybody with him. That's why he killed him."

"Who killed who?" Roger inquired.

"Mike Eiffert killed Brian Stensler."

"Now, why would he do that?"

"The whole plan was Mike Eiffert's. He contacted me a couple of months ago and he brought up this idea of how we could get a little bump and the insurance company would probably never find out as long as we weren't too greedy."

As he spoke, Roger Legion recalled that Mike had contacted him several times via email over that time period to offer help for any problems Roger may have.

"Mike Eiffert believes that you killed Brian Stensler," Roger told him.

"That's a lie! All three of us were at my apartment and Mike stormed out after he and Brian got into it. Then Brian left. Next morning I heard Brian was killed. I never left my apartment."

"Then why did you run?" Legion demanded.

"If Mike Eiffert knew where to find me, he would have killed me next. That guy has ice for blood running through his veins."

"So Mike was the guy who came up with this whole idea to steal from Unibility Insurance."

"Yes," Ned answered concisely.

"Let me ask you this now. Did I have anything to do with stealing money from Unibility Insurance or did anyone else at this law firm other than Brian Stensler, Mike Eiffert, and you?" Legion spoke like an interrogator at a deposition.

"Nah, well, no," Ned stumbled through his words.

"SAY IT!" Legion flared.

"Neither Roger Legion, nor anyone at his firm, other than myself, Brian Stensler, and Mike Eiffert were involved in our," Ned paused for a moment, "scheme to defraud Unibility Insurance by sending phony invoices."

Brian realized that he had just confessed to a major crime.

"Where are you?" Legion queried.

"Roger, you're going to help me with this, right?" Ned begged.

"How can I help you if I don't know where you are? The police are looking for you. Do you want my help or not?" Legion's voice was definitive.

"You're not going to sell me out, are you?" Ned pleaded with a tone of sadness in his voice.

"I won't let them touch you," Legion assured him. "I won't allow this law firm to be besmirched. Now, where are you?"

"Let me call you back," Ned answered quickly and ended the call.

Roger returned the phone to its cradle. He now understood Mike Eiffert's desire to be his partner. If Legion was found guilty of a crime, he would lose his law license and be forced to sell his interest in the firm. Mike Eiffert would be left to run it.

Legion needed a plan to straighten out this latest wrinkle. And it was about to step off the elevator.

CHAPTER 75

When FBI Special Agent Brenda Tomaras left Daisy Zacaro's office, she toyed with the idea of going to the local FBI office, located approximately fifteen miles to the north in the Sorrento Mesa area of the city, but she ultimately passed on the idea. She feared that she would receive orders telling her to stop any involvement in San Diego with the Mondo Run robbery.

Brenda sauntered back to the America's Finest City Building and found herself in the America's Finest City News store. It was a convenience store located on the first floor of the building that also sold a wide variety of newspapers and magazines.

She looked on the wall at the various assortment of magazines and her eyes were drawn to two magazines involving puzzles. One was called, *Figure It Out,* and the other was called, *Racecar Backwards.* The second book dealt with word games, such as palindromes and anagrams.

Brenda reached for the *Racecar Backwards* magazine and her hand stopped suddenly in mid-air. She experienced a moment of revelation, which sent her out of the store and directly to the elevators for the twenty-fourth floor.

After a non-stop ride to Legion & Associates, Brenda stepped off the elevator and Nina was not sitting at her reception desk. A small, folded cardboard placeholder was perched on her counter that said, 'Be Right Back!'

Special Agent Tomaras walked directly to Legion's office and looked inside while he sat at his desk in full contemplative mode. She knocked.

"Hello, Special Agent Brenda," Legion responded to her knock. "I forgot your last name."

"Tomaras," she replied.

"Come on in."

Legion rose from his chair as she entered the room.

"I'm sorry, but there was no one at the reception desk," she stated.

"That happens," Legion conceded. "How can I help you?"

"Mr. Legion, I asked you earlier if you knew George Lorin. And you said, 'No,' is that correct?"

"That's right, I don't recognize that name."

"I was just at the office of your Assistant Attorney General, Daisy something," Brenda shared.

"Lucky you," Legion responded sarcastically. "You can take that off your bucket list."

"She ordered the other FBI officers to draft an arrest warrant for you for the robbery that took place outside of Sandpoint, Idaho. Now, I think you're being set-up Mr. Legion and I want to help you, but you've got to help me. Here," she said handing him a piece of paper with two words on it. "Take a look at it."

He did. The words were 'George Lorin.' Legion again looked at Brenda.

"Okay?" he answered, wondering what she wanted him to say.

"George Lorin was the guy identified as the person who pulled off an armored truck heist for more than five million dollars, known as the Mondo Run. That day he murdered two Idaho state troopers, the three-member crew of the armored truck, three accomplices who helped him plan the heist and subsequently four members of his own crew, who helped him pull it off. Twelve people in all. George Lorin used a bomb similar to the one found in your trunk to stop the armored truck and those money bands, found in your trunk, can be tied directly to the robbery."

"You're right," Legion replied with indignity. "I am being set-up."

"Now," Brenda again began, "if Daisy has her way, they will be crucifying you before the end of the day. I want to help you, but you've got to help me. Take a look at that name again."

Legion again looked at it and then looked back at her.

"George Lorin is an anagram," she told him. "For Roger Legion."

Legion slowly lowered his head to look at the piece of paper to confirm that she was correct. A shroud of silence enveloped the room. The silence was broken by Brenda's voice.

"Do you know who robbed that armored truck outside of Sandpoint, Idaho?"

"I do now," he uttered, realizing the depths of Mike Eiffert's betrayal.

CHAPTER 76

Special Agents Pete Chrisman and Bob Malloy returned to Assistant US Attorney Daisy Zacaro's office at an appointed time to meet regarding service of an arrest warrant on Roger Legion. Pete Chrisman had prepared the warrant and Daisy had one of her Orange County judicial friends sign it. The three of them left her office for a short walk to the America's Finest City Building. Not a word was spoken among them for the three block walk.

At approximately the same time, a red, Ford, late-model transit van, from a company called Bay Valet Detail, parked in a loading zone on the eastern side of the America's Finest City Building. This company dry-cleaned clothes and provided personal delivery and pickup. In addition, they also detailed vehicles. Their motto was 'We Clean Cars & Clothes!'

All of the male employees of Bay Valet Detail wore an outfit that looked like a tuxedo without the suitcoat. They wore black pants with shiny black piping down the side. A vest with a cummerbund, white long-sleeve shirt, cufflinks, and a clip-on bow tie.

The driver of the van was short and slender, balding and clean-shaven. He exited the van and slid a sliding side-door back.

He then set up a small ramp from the van to the sidewalk. From the van, he slid down a rolling clothes rail. This device was six feet high with a clothes bar hanger running down the center of the top of it. The hanging clothes were covered by a large, black, garment bag-type covering with Bay Valet Detail's logo on it.

When the rolling clothes rail was on the sidewalk, the Bay Valet Detail employee closed the van and locked it before proceeding into the building.

At Legion & Associates, Roger Legion sat at his desk typing an email. When he wanted one of his attorneys to make an appearance in his office, he would send them a simple email that said, 'Come to my office. ASAP.' He would use the same email over and over.

Mike Eiffert sat reviewing a deposition for an upcoming trial when he noticed that he was summoned by one of Roger's famous emails. He stopped what he was doing immediately and sprinted to his office. Mike rapped on his door.

"Come on in," Roger said accompanied by a fast wave.

"What's going on?" Mike wondered with a carefree smile.

"I've got your partnership contract here," Roger told him. "I didn't want you to think I forgot."

"There's no rush on this," Mike shared. "With all the stuff that's been going on around here, we've got bigger fish to fry."

"That we do," Roger added. "You want to call your wife and tell her?"

Mike looked at him with an odd smirk.

"Nah, she's busy," Mike replied.

"I heard they just found your mother-in-law." Roger's tone was becoming ominous. "Lisa Ruff. They found her body in some abandoned cabin. Hacked up. Are you sure you don't want to call your wife, because they're looking for her now and your daughter."

Mike shook his head in a negative motion.

"How about George Lorin?" Legion asked. "You want to call him? Interesting anagram for Roger Legion, don't you think?"

Mike was flummoxed and let out a sigh.

"A great man," Mike began. "A GREAT man," he repeated with indignation, "once taught me how to get rid of bad facts. You do it through displacement, misplacement, or replacement. So, I used that life lesson to do what I had to do."

"Does that include stealing my law firm?" Legion quizzed.

"No. I have too much respect for you. I would never have done any of this unless I knew that you could beat it."

"All they would have to do Mike is tag me on one thing. Then I'd lose my law license and I wouldn't be allowed to be a partner in the firm. I'd have to walk away."

"After you're bought out," Mike added. "But I know you can beat it all."

"I don't know. You got me involved with this Unibility Insurance thing and now, this, this robbery in Idaho."

"Roger, you're forgetting about the Judge. Remember. His car went boom!"

When he uttered the last word, both of his hands popped open.

"Why did you pull off that robbery anyway?" Roger wondered.

"Montana is a desolate wasteland. You have a lot of time to think. And me, well, I like to think big."

"Why did you kill so many people?" Legion wondered.

"Roger, would you like me to sign a confession?" Mike responded. His face then filled with a sinister smile. "Come on out, Sparkplug," Mike spoke toward the doorway. "I know you're there.

I smelled your perfume when I walked in. Ferragamo's 'F' for Fascinating. The Night version."

Brenda pushed the door and leveled her Smith & Wesson M & P .40 caliber semi-automatic pistol at him with both hands.

"Don't move. Keep your hands where I can see them," she warned.

"Hey, Sparkplug. The eye is healing up nicely," Mike told her with a sarcastic grin.

"Mr. Legion, would you call the local FBI office and tell them I have a suspect for transport," Brenda asked.

"I'm afraid," Mike cautioned, "that Mr. Legion can't do that. Can you, Mr. Legion?"

Roger looked at Mike and didn't move. Brenda gazed upon Legion with a visage of shock. She had one question for Legion.

"Don't tell me you were involved with him in the robbery?"

Meanwhile, the employee from the Bay Valet Detail took his wheeled clothesline to the seventh floor of the building. This floor was unoccupied and he wheeled it slightly down the hallway and unzipped one side of the garment-type bag to allow Otto Stern out of the wheeled device.

Stern stood up, wearing the exact same black suit he wore when he last visited Roger Legion and murdered San Diego Police detective Pete Atherton. He brushed his clothes, then reached into the garment bag to pull out a .380 Walther semi-automatic pistol. He placed it behind him in his waistband.

Otto then pulled out a small device that looked like a garage door opener. The Bay Valet Detail employee also had one.

"Red," Otto said, referring to a small light on the device, "come and get me. If it's green, I'll meet you at the van."

Otto Stern moved back to the elevators and called for a car.

Special Agents Pete Chrisman, Bob Malloy, and Assistant Attorney General Daisy Zacaro were on their way to the twenty-fourth floor, when the elevator they were in stopped at the twenty-third floor. Daisy saw the logo for Legion & Associates and stepped off the elevator. Both of the Special Agents stepped off with her and Pete shared a comment.

"This is the wrong floor."

"Why didn't you say something, asshole? Christ almighty! The only thing I can count on from you guys is disappointment. Where's the stairs!?"

Bob Malloy held the door to the stairway open for her and they began their ascent to the next floor.

In Roger Legion's office, Roger shook his head in a negative manner in response to Brenda's question regarding his involvement in the Mondo Run robbery. Brenda wondered why Legion was being exceptionally quiet.

"What are you going to do, Sparkplug?" Mike Eiffert asked.

"I am arresting you for robbery and first degree murder," she informed him.

"Who's got the time?" Mike asked and no one looked for a clock. "You should call your daughter, Brenda. Make sure she got home today."

"No," she retorted. "You're bluffing. I know because I'm smart and you're stupid."

As she spoke, Brenda moved her body farther into the office, so she was not blocking the doorway. Mike Eiffert eyeballed her up and down.

"Mr. Legion taught me a long time ago never to be afraid. It's a wasted emotion. He also taught me to capitalize on the fear of your opponent. I know you won't shoot me, but I also know you're afraid that I'm going to kill you. BOO!"

Brenda did a slight kneejerk reaction to Mike's utterance of the word, 'Boo.' He immediately slapped her gun to one side sending it into the corner of the room and followed it up with a roundhouse punch to Brenda's face. Mike took off like a man on fire, out of the office racing down the hallway. Brenda sprung to her feet, with blood dripping from her left nostril, and took off after him without her weapon.

Roger picked up the gun in high pursuit of Brenda.

In the reception area, a bell went off indicating that the center elevator had arrived. At just about the same time, Pete Chrisman, Bob Malloy, and Daisy Zacaro reached the twenty-fourth floor. They entered through a staircase door located at the far left end of the elevator banks.

The doors of the center elevator opened and Otto Stern emerged. In his grand Aryan style, he walked directly to the receptionist counter to announce his arrival to Nina.

Nina appeared to be looking down at her desk and only the crown of her head was visible. But it was not Nina sitting at the reception desk. It was Margaret Byrne.

On the desktop, she had two weapons: her Sig Sauer, 9 mm, semi-automatic pistol and a Kimber 9 mm Onyx Ultra. Each gun was filled with ten hollow-point bullets in the magazine and the hammers were cocked back with a bullet in the chambers. She slipped her hands into the grips and her index fingers onto the triggers.

She watched for the elevator door to close with only a slit of her eyes over the granite countertop. When it did, Margaret stood immediately and her chair rolled back to the wall. As she stood, her arms extended and the guns murderously roared to life. Margaret wanted to make sure that each pull of the trigger was a kill shot.

When the gunfire started, the door to the elevator on the far right had opened and was closing just as Mike Eiffert was approaching. Margaret's gunfire did not seem to faze him. He slid into the elevator just as the door was closing.

Margaret saw Brenda and Legion were tearing down the hallway in pursuit of Mike. Brenda was visibly upset that he was going to get away. Legion immediately tapped Brenda on the shoulder with one hand and returned the handgun to her.

"OPEN THE DOORS!" Margaret screamed.

Candelario or Candy, the man who worked in the Transport Systems department of the building was listening to all the events from Margaret's cellphone. As soon as she screamed the command, the door to the elevator where Mike Eiffert was hiding opened. He stood there and locked eyes with Brenda. A wailing sound was coming from the elevator at the other end. Without thought, Brenda instantly leveled her gun and shot at him once, in the center of his mass and he slammed against the back wall of the elevator. And then, like a computer-guided missile, she raised the gun six more inches. A second bullet between his eyes blew off the back of his skull, splattering the back wall of the elevator with blood and brain matter. Mike Eiffert's lifeless body crumpled to the floor.

When Margaret called out for the doors to be opened, there was no car in the far left elevator bank. That car was on the twenty-eighth floor. When Margaret began her fusillade of bullets into Otto Stern, both Special Agents shielded Daisy against the first elevator door, while they drew their weapons to determine if they were going to return fire. When Margaret ordered the doors opened, a special alarm went off indicating that there was no car at one of the elevator banks. Once the Special Agents saw Brenda level her weapon, they took a shooting position that accidentally tapped Daisy with their butts. She lost her balance and fell down the elevator shaft.

Both Pete and Bob could hear her scream on the way down. They both turned toward each other. Pete held out his fist and Bob bumped it.

All of this happened in the ten to twelve seconds it took for Margaret to empty twenty bullets into Otto Stern. He had turned back to the elevator and pulled his gun out, but her blitzkrieg shredded his body. There was one bloody handprint on the elevator call buttons that dragged down the wall. That was the last request Otto Stern ever made.

The elevator warning siren continued to blare. Margaret's guns had their slides pulled back indicating they were empty. The smell of gunpowder filled the air and white smoke rose from the barrels of her guns.

She set the Kimber gun down on the granite countertop as she walked around the reception desk and dropped the empty clip from her Sig Sauer pistol. Margaret slapped a full magazine into it and released the slide. That stripped the first bullet into the chamber, ready to commence firing again if necessary.

When the gun was ready to fire, she re-aimed at Otto Stern, who was most definitely dead. Margaret walked over to view Brenda's handiwork. Margaret looked at Brenda and Brenda looked at her. Brenda then wiped the blood from her nose, using the sleeve of her blazer.

From her pocket, Margaret retrieved a handkerchief. She reached behind her back, under her red blazer, and using the handkerchief, she retrieved a .38 caliber, snub-nosed revolver, also referred to as a 'Saturday Night Special.' Margaret was going to use it as a drop gun in the event Otto Stern was not armed. She handed the gun, covered by the handkerchief to Brenda.

Brenda took the gun and continued to wipe it as she stepped into the elevator with Mike Eiffert's dead body. She placed the gun into his right hand, including the placement of his index finger on the trigger. Brenda then stepped out of the elevator.

Within seconds, a barrage of police officers flooded the twenty-fourth floor.

The only person to witness all the events, other than those people actively involved in them, was Roger Legion.

CHAPTER 77

Four days after the confluence of violence and the death of Crazy Daisy Zacaro, Glenn Edgarian appeared in the reception area of Legion & Associates. Glenn perused the wall and the elevators. He could see no damage to the walls or elevators and they were sparkling clean.

Glenn had just returned from his unscheduled trip to Santa Isabella, Mexico, nearly nine hundred miles from downtown San Diego. He was held in a small, local jail, awaiting a prison transport. Glenn was told that he signed a confession that he was a drug runner and was sentenced to twenty-two years in a federal prison near Mexico City.

"I'm here to see the big guy," Glenn told Nina with his million dollar smile.

"He's in his office. I'll let him know you're on your way," she shared with her bright smile.

Before Glenn could knock on Legion's door, he heard a voice.

"Come on in," Roger told him and stood from his chair. Instead of the usual firm handshake, they met each other with a quick hug and took a step back from each other.

"It's good to see you. All I'm going to say is 'Thank you,'" Glenn told him.

"Don't worry about it," Roger answered with a smile. "Have a seat."

"I really thought my ass was in a salad shooter down there," Glenn confided. "They drugged me, took my contact lenses, said I confessed to being a drug runner, and I agreed to a sentence of twenty-two years in prison."

"Crazy Daisy was always real thorough," Roger shared.

"Here's the skinny on that bitch," Glenn began. "Zacaro was her married name. About ten years ago, she was married for nine months, but kept the name afterwards. Her maiden name was Reynolds. She had one brother and he was a lawyer. Mark Reynolds."

Roger took a moment to soak in that information. Mark Reynolds was a Legion lawyer who died in the famous conference room firefight of five years earlier. But what only Roger Legion and Mike Eiffert knew was that Mark had murdered a claims manager at Acitu Mutual Insurance and another Legion lawyer named Ted Theopolis.

"Wow," Roger said. "I did not see that coming."

"Oh, it gets better. Shortly before the famous conference room massacre, Crazy Daisy was pregnant. The baby was stillborn about a week before. According to the Fetal Death Certificate, the father was listed as Mark Reynolds. So, brother and sister were a little tighter than usual."

Roger leaned back in his chair and shook his head.

"Well, now I understand why she went through all the hoops to prevent you from finding this out." He smiled at Glenn. "Don't forget to put the cost of the contacts on the bill. And this time, I want you to add five thousand dollars to your bill. Send it over and I'll get it paid today."

"This time," Glenn advised, "I'm not going to argue with you. I guess I should stay out of Mexico for the rest of my life."

"No. That will all be taken care of. I would avoid it for maybe the next six months."

"Where did you find that guy, Joe the Lawyer?" Glenn wondered.

"A friend of a friend," Roger replied.

Glenn stood from his chair and this time he did share a firm handshake with Roger Legion.

"I've got to ask you," Glenn wondered. "That whole deal with Daisy going down the elevator shaft, Mike Eiffert, and the guy who killed the cop. Was it like the conference room five years ago?"

Roger looked at Glenn and thought about his question for a moment.

"No, it was nothing like that. That was a moment of victory. This time, I believe it was more like what a lawyer must experience when they lose in court."

Glenn acknowledged his response, realizing that Roger Legion had no idea what it was like to lose in court.

"Take care, my friend," Glenn shared as he left Legion's office.

Legion turned to gaze at the ocean and thought about the time he told a room of attorneys that Mike Eiffert should be Lawyer of the Year. Roger was having a difficult time comprehending how Mike could go from that to how he ended up.

CHAPTER 78

Approximately ninety miles from downtown San Diego, in the San Jacinto Valley of Riverside County lies the city of Hemet, California. Since it was incorporated in 1910, this twenty-seven square mile city was primarily the trading center for the area's agriculture, which included citrus, apricots, peaches, olives, and walnuts.

Large scale residential development began in the 1960s and Hemet earned a reputation as a working-class retirement area. Its rural nature made it attractive to families that were priced out of other areas of Southern California.

Near the corner of West Acacia Avenue and North Kirby Street was situated the Limberlost Cabins Motel. Built in the early 1960s, this motel suffered from years of neglect that could not be corrected with a simple coat of paint. Yet, it maintained a loyal clientele for its rustic cabin motif and the management's desire not to become involved with its guests.

Ned Chandler entered Cabin 18, where he had been staying for the past three days. Five days earlier, he spoke with Roger Legion and asked him for help because he feared Mike Eiffert was going to kill him. Now, with Mike Eiffert dead, he was slightly at ease, but not much. He knew the police were looking for him to question him regarding the death of his co-conspirator in the

Unibility larceny scheme, Brian Stensler, and his running was not going to help his case.

It was 9:30 at night and Ned was returning from a Denny's for his only meal of the day. When he entered the cabin, he flicked a switch, closest to the door, but the light did not come on. This was not unusual and he walked farther into the cabin to turn on one of two lights located over the beds.

As he turned on the light, he heard the door to the cabin close. Ned turned quickly and he locked eyes with a man, who was six feet tall, with a lean, but solid build, wearing jeans, a white button shirt, unbuttoned at the neck, a black sport coat, and black Stetson hat. It was Joe the Lawyer.

In his hand, he held a 9 mm Berretta FS with a sound suppressor or silencer screwed on to the end of the barrel.

Ned's eyes moved from the gun to the eyes of the gunman.

"Hey man," Ned pleaded holding his hands around the height of his chest. "Take it easy."

"Roger Legion says 'Hello.'"

Joe swiftly leveled the gun and shot Ned once in the head. The muffled sound of the gun was still loud, but not enough to cause any outsider's concern. Ned's body hit one of the beds and bounced off and onto the floor.

Joe then put a second bullet in him to make sure that his assignment was complete.

EPILOGUE

Downtown San Diego
51 Weeks Later

The distance between the America's Finest City Building and the San Diego Hall of Justice, which was the newer courthouse, was only three blocks. Yet, Roger Legion could hardly walk it without someone saying, 'Hello,' or wanting to talk. He would always stop to talk unless he was running late for a court appearance.

This day would be no exception. Roger left the courthouse after attending a Case Management Conference. As he waited for the pedestrian crosswalk light to turn green at the corner of Broadway and State Street, a voice called out his name.

"Roger," the young lady said as she lightly took hold of his arm.

He turned and there stood Margaret Byrne. Her hair was pulled back and held in place with a hairband. She wore a white dress with a red and black floral print, along with a black cardigan button sweater.

Roger had not seen her since that day when she killed Otto Stern in Legion's reception area. Margaret had been surveilling the Bay Valet Detail van and Legion assisted in sneaking her into the building.

Margaret received a Medal of Valor for her work in apprehending the killer of San Diego Detective Pete Atherton.

"Hello, Margaret," Roger told her with a smile. "How are you?"

"I'm fine, Roger. How about you?"

"I'm good. Keeping busy."

"I'm leaving the police force," she shared.

"Oh, really. What are you going to do?"

"I don't know," Margaret replied. "Maybe private investigation or maybe law school. Would you give me a job?" she asked with a raised eyebrow and a wry smile.

"I'd have to think about that," Roger answered with a doubtful look and a smile.

"I had lunch with Brenda Tomaras last week. Can you believe next week will be a year?"

"How's she doing?" Roger wondered and acknowledged her comment.

"They're going to make her Special Agent-in-Charge of the Coeur d'Alene office," Margaret told him.

For her work in catching and stopping Michael Eiffert, also known as George Lorin, the perpetrator of the Mondo Run robbery and attendant murders, Brenda received the FBI Medal for Meritorious Achievement.

"That's great," Roger declared. "She deserves it."

"Imagine if they knew what really happened?"

STOP!

Did Margaret just say, 'what really happened?' She did. And Legion began to remember.

As Brenda chased Mike Eiffert down the hallway, Legion chased her, while carrying Brenda's Smith & Wesson M & P .40 caliber semi-automatic pistol.

As Legion reached the reception area, Margaret was in the process of standing from the chair to a full upright position. In that moment, Otto Stern recognized her and started to scream.

"DON'T SHOOT! DON'T SHOOT!"

But it made no difference. Margaret was not there that day for mercy. She was there to impose the death penalty. Even though Otto Stern was probably dead with the second bullet, she pumped a torrent of eighteen more bullets into him for what he did to her partner.

Margaret did see Mike Eiffert slide into the elevator to the right just as the door was closing, she did yell for the doors to be open. Because there was no elevator car at the elevator to the left, a blaring warning siren went off. Special Agents Pete Chrisman and Bob Malloy were initially shielding Daisy Zacaro during Margaret's burst of gunfire.

Once the elevator doors opened to the elevator shaft, Daisy screamed, "Get out of the way, assholes!"

The Special Agents did not move, but rather pivoted toward each other and in the same move, they both shoved Daisy with one hand each into the elevator shaft. Her screams could be heard for nearly the entire twenty-four floor drop.

Mike Eiffert thought that he had successfully eluded Brenda Tomaras when his elevator door closed. When the door opened, Mike Eiffert stood there with his eyes locked with Roger Legion.

"MIKE!" Legion screamed and Mike stared at him in the moment, like a child trying to be obedient to their father.

In a nanosecond, Legion leveled the gun and shot Mike in the center of the chest. Mike stared at him in shocked disbelief as if a father had just shot his son. Legion immediately handed the gun to Brenda, grip first, and she held it on Mike with both arms extended. He made a quick, slouch movement down the elevator wall and Brenda put a second bullet between his eyes that blew off the back of his head.

Margaret did give Brenda the drop gun, which she placed in Mike Eiffert's hand before any other police arrived.

Roger Legion had not thought about that day for a long time. It was less than a month before, when Roger found out that the Federal government dropped their inquiry into the Unibility Insurance fraudulent billings after hearing Ned Chandler's confession and all the money was returned.

Margaret asked Roger if he would like to go to lunch sometime and he agreed. She said that she would call him in the next week.

Roger walked back to the America's Finest City Building and requested a non-stop elevator to the twenty-fourth floor. As the doors to the elevator opened, he thought about Mike Eiffert and the reason that he had to pull the trigger that day.

While she held a gun on Mike Eiffert in Legion's office, Brenda asked Roger to call the local FBI office for backup help. Mike Eiffert assuredly told Brenda that Roger would not call anyone.

Roger and Mike planned the car bombing of State Superior Court Judge Harrison Ogilvie. If the police were to get ahold of Mike Eiffert, Roger would have a serious problem. Legion could not take that chance.

Shortly after the elevator bloodshed, Roger Legion drove out to a storage unit in El Centro, California, located one hundred thirteen miles to the east in Imperial County. Mike Eiffert told Roger, after giving him a key, that if anything ever happened to him, the stuff in the storage unit would be Roger's property.

Roger arrived at the storage unit unrecognizable, wearing jeans, a t-shirt, and a baseball cap. Inside the unit were three wooden crates, approximately four by three feet wide, and four feet high. Roger used the tire iron from his car to pry the top off of one of the crates. The crates contained the money from the Mondo Run robbery.

Roger had the money shipped to an acquaintance who was able to launder it and provide Legion with nearly five million dollars of 'clean' funds. Roger took the money and established a non-profit charitable organization for the children of Legion lawyers. Money would be used to pay for education, medical expenses, and housing to help a child of any of his lawyers afford life in San Diego. Roger did this with the hope that it would minimize the greed factor and prevent his lawyers from seeking out easy money. He did not want to add any more names to the Memorial Plaque.

One final note: According to the autopsy report of Daisy Zacaro, the medical examiner stated that a word was carved into the pubic area of her body. The word was 'Neco.' A Latin word meaning kill, murder, slay, or put to death.

<u>JOE THE LAWYER</u>

This is a story that's mostly true,
Except for the parts I'm telling you.
I knew a guy, his name was Joe,
He said he was a lawyer from Mexico.
(Whoa-ooh-ooh-ooh-oh-oh-oh)

Joe did time in Tennessee.
He said it was for murder, first degree.
I asked Joe where he learned the law.
He said it was a bar in Wichita.
 (Whoa-ooh-ooh-ooh-oh-oh-oh)

He liked to rob and he liked to steal.
Just like lawyers cuttin' deals.
Joe said his training served him well
At least as far as he could tell.
(Whoa-ooh-ooh-ooh-oh-oh-oh)

      Is there law in Mexico?
      Don't ask me, I don't know.
      Joe said down there they do it right
      They just kill everybody in sight.
      Why be a lawyer in Mexico?
      Don't ask me, I don't know.

Joe had a girl, her name was Jill,
She liked to drive and she loved to kill.
One day when they stopped for smokes
She wouldn't pay and shot those folks.

(Whoa-ooh-ooh-ooh-oh-oh-oh)

Jill thought the trial was kinda fair.
Joe was her lawyer and she got the chair.
Joe asked her to be his wife.
Last I heard, she was doing life.
(Whoa-ooh-ooh-ooh-oh-oh-oh)

Is there law in Mexico?
Don't ask me, I don't know.
Joe said down there they do it right
They just kill everybody in sight.
Why be a lawyer in Mexico?
Don't ask me, I don't know.

The only two things that you gotta know,
Is hold a gun and do some blow.
There's no trial, no appeal.
No rat's that are gonna squeal.
If you wanna roll in dough,
You better be a lawyer from Mexico.
(Whoa-ooh-ooh-ooh-oh-oh-oh)

Joe got stopped in Abilene.
That big prick was pretty mean.
Joe shot him in the head.
Rest in peace, he was dead.
(Whoa-ooh-ooh-ooh-oh-oh-oh)

They got Joe in a bar one night.
Cops shot him with delight.
There's one thing that they oughta know.
They just shot a lawyer from Mexico

VINCE AIELLO

(Whoa-ooh-ooh-ooh-oh-oh-oh)

Is there law in Mexico?
Don't ask me, I don't know.
Joe said down there they do it right
They just kill everybody in sight.
Why be a lawyer in Mexico?
Don't ask me, I don't know.

Well, that's the story of my friend, Joe.
He was a lawyer from Mexico.
Ask Joe if he'd do it again.
You say where, and he'd say when.
Joe said he was always told,
There's no point in growing old.
He just did what lawyers do.
Made a life out of screwing you.
(Whoa-ooh-ooh-ooh-oh-oh-oh)

The only two things that you gotta know,
Is hold a gun and do some blow.
There's no trial, no appeal.
No rat's that are gonna squeal.
If you wanna roll in dough,
You better be a lawyer from Mexico.
(Whoa-ooh-ooh-ooh-oh-oh-oh)

Is there law in Mexico?
Don't ask me, I don't know.
Joe said down there they do it right
They just kill everybody in sight.
Why be a lawyer in Mexico?
Don't ask me, I don't know.

I don't know.
I don't know.

Adios, Joe. (Spoken)

Available on YouTube® and Amazon.com

About the Author

Vince Aiello grew up in upstate New York before moving to Southern California where he attended California Western School of Law. He is admitted to practice law in both New York and California. *Lethal Equity* is his fifth novel. His earlier novels, *Legal Detriment*, *The Litigation Guy*, *Legion's Lawyers* and *Faith Full* were all acclaimed bestsellers. Visit his website at www.vinceaiello.com.

ACKNOWLEDGEMENTS

I would like to thank the following individuals for providing support and, in some instances, the use of their name for a fictional character in *Lethal Equity*:

Ethan P. Aiello
Sarah Rose Aiello
Valerie R. Aiello, RPh
Margaret Byrne, Esq.
Paul Clifford
Glenn Edgarian
Michael Eiffert, M.D.
Nina Eiffert
Angelo Garubo, Esq.
Troy Geisser, Esq.
Lisa Leffort Reynolds
Mark Reynolds
Elisa Ruff
Brenda Tomaras, Esq.

www.ingramcontent.com/pod-product-compliance
Lightning Source LLC
Chambersburg PA
CBHW070834250626
47159CB00003B/775